REVENGE:
THE
SWEETEST
JOY

VIV LOVE

Printed in the United States of America.
ISBN: 978-0-9982706-4-7
First Printing, 2019
www.valpughlove.com
Shreveport, LA 71109

This book is dedicated to the dreamers and believers.
Keep pushing. Make it happen.

Queen V

PROLOGUE

Sisterly Love

"Hey, sis. It's handled," Cheyenne said to Vivian seconds after she slit Marissa's throat.

Cheyenne and Marissa had been friends and business partners for more than a decade. Their friendship was more like a sisterhood. They shared things with each other that they'd never told anyone else. These two ladies had been through so much together, which is why it was so hard for Cheyenne to stomach the thought of Marissa plotting with anyone to kill her – especially with Cheyenne's own brother. While Cheyenne has always been the least violent member of her family, she knew there was no way she could allow Marissa to live another day. So, under the direction of her big sis, Vivian, she murdered her best friend.

"Great. Did anyone see you enter the shop?" Vivian asked.

"No. I parked down the street as you instructed, and I entered through the back door."

"What about the alarm system? Was it armed when you arrived?" Vivian shot question after question to ensure Cheyenne had covered her tracks.

"No. I didn't arm it when I left last night. I also made sure the internet modem was offline so that the alarm system would not monitor any activity," Cheyenne replied nervously.

The stillness in Vivian's voice made her feel like she was being interrogated by the cops.

"Great. Exit the same way you entered. Make sure no one sees you. The crew will take care of the rest."

"Okay," Cheyenne replied.

"One last thing," Vivian said before hanging up the phone. "Welcome to the dark side."

As Vivian stood at her favorite spot overlooking downtown Shreveport, her phone vibrated in her hand. She answered without looking, expecting it to be Cheyenne calling right back.

"Yes, ma'am."

"Queen, we have a problem."

She looked at her phone to check the name of the caller. She was a bit startled to hear Paul's voice on the other end. He was one of the guys from the cleanup crew at the Queendom.

"What kind of problem?" she asked.

"It seems one of them is still alive. The woman is still alive. Do you want me to finish the job?"

"How could that be possible? She was shot in the head. I witnessed it myself. What makes you think she's alive?"

"She was moving and moaning when I came in to get her and her husband so that I could dispose of their bodies. She keeps asking to speak with you. What do you want me to do? I've already put her husband in the incinerator. Should I throw her in as well?"

Paul was savage and took great care of Vivian in a big brother kind of way. She never had to worry about a job being left undone if he was taking care of it.

"No… That won't be necessary. Call Nurse Dawn and have to her examine Ava. I'll be there shortly," Vivian said as she hung up the phone with Paul and gathered her things to head to the Queendom.

CHAPTER ONE
CHEYENNE

New Me, Who Dis?

After killing Marissa, I thought I would feel weird or paranoid, but I actually feel better than I've ever felt before. For the first time in my life, I stood up for myself and followed through with the threats of "Respect me or else." Marissa got her "or else" and VJ will get his punishment in due time. I finally have the relationship with my parents and sister that I've longed for my whole life. I have a newfound energy as if I could conquer the world right now. While I identify as female, I still scope the scene to hang with other members of the LGBTQ+ community. Lately, I've had my eye on an ex-NBA player who recently returned home due to an injury of his Achilles tendon.

When I first saw him on the night that the gays typically frequent my favorite nightclub, I was shocked and didn't think it was him. Then, I remembered the rumors that he was caught leaving the room of one of his teammates late one night. I assumed they'd had a party or a few girls over. However, my source suggested that the two of them were alone, and my prospect was seen fixing his clothes and wiping his mouth as he exited the room. Now that I've seen him in the club several times, I believe there's far more truth to those rumors.

My crew and I like to frequent Thirsty Thursdays at Metropolis because the event is hosted by the best DJ in the city. It was originally a gay club, but now the crowd is a mixture of business professionals, party-goers, straight folks, and queer folks. The vibe is mad lit all night. I decided to go the night after I killed Marissa to take my mind off the events of the week. As I sat on a stool at the end of the bar vibing to the music and watching the crowd, someone at the other end of the bar sent a drink to me. When my favorite bartender, Elisa, told me I had a secret admirer, I expected it to be some old worn-down man who wanted me to fulfill a fantasy he'd kept hidden from his family for years. That's typically the type of guy that sends me drinks. I was pleasantly surprised to look up and see Hakeem, the ex-NBA star smiling slyly at me.

"Girl, are you sure *he* sent it?" I asked Elisa as I tried to avoid making eye contact with Hakeem.

"Yes, ma'am. He also sent his name and number. So what cha going to do?"

"I'm going to guzzle this drink and shoot him a text," I said as I quickly downed the best Cosmopolitan that I'd ever tasted in my life. When I turned around to place my martini glass on the bar, I noticed that Hakeem was still staring at me. This time, he smiled and flashed the brightest, whitest teeth in the building. His smile was complemented by two deep dimples, a full set of juicy lips, and a thick beard that covered smooth milk chocolate skin. He was dark enough to be from the motherland and light enough to taste like caramel. Without hesitation, I grabbed my cell from my clutch and shot him a text.

"Thanks for the drink."

Then, I gripped my phone in my hand and waited for him to reply. I pretended to scan the crowd as I watched him from my peripheral. I saw him look at his phone and smile. I just knew he'd respond to my message, but he didn't. Instead, he slid his phone back in his pocket and made his way through the crowd. This gesture was baffling, so I turned to Elisa to clarify that the sexy specimen I'd been watching was the same person who sent me the drink.

"Fish, get your ass over here!" I scolded.

"I told you about calling me Fish, heffa. What's the problem?" Elisa asked, playfully rolling her eyes.

"Girl, are you sure the fine dude with the beard and dimples sent me that drink and number?"

"Yeah. Why do you ask?"

"Well, I sent him a text. I think he read it. But the strangest thing happened next. I assumed he'd text back or make his way toward me. Instead, this negro just smiled, put the phone back in his pocket, and left."

"What do you mean *left*?"

"He walked through the crowd toward the exit. I couldn't really see him anymore, but I know that's the direction he was headed. He can't tease me like that," I said disappointedly.

"Maybe he suddenly got shy," Elisa suggested. "Give him a minute to text you back. If he doesn't text in the next few days. Just let it go."

I nodded my head in agreement and turned back around to resume watching the crowd move and sway to DJ Money Cha$er as he played all the hottest hits. I tried to act like I wasn't disappointed in Hakeem's actions, but I couldn't help but think about him. *Did I seem too thirsty? Did I guzzle my drink too fast and turn him off? Should I have waited to text him?* I asked myself question after question and began to doubt myself as usual. Just as I grabbed my clutch and turned to tell Elisa that I was heading home. I felt a soft tap on my shoulder. When I turned around, I was face-to-face with none other than Hakeem himself.

Although the club was filled with the scent of cigars, marijuana, and alcohol, I was still intoxicated by the invigorating scent of Invictus cologne that captured my olfactory senses. I could have melted right on that bar stool. I finally found my voice and managed a slow and sensual, "H-hi."

"Hello," he responded in the sexiest baritone voice. "I'm Hakeem. You're welcome."

"Welcome?" I asked, drawing a blank because of the hypnosis he had on me.

"For the drink. This is my response to your text. Sorry I didn't text back. I wanted to tell you in person."

Embarrassed, I cleared my throat and tried to restrain my smile before I replied, "Oh, yeah the drink. I forgot I sent the text message. Well, thanks for responding, Hakeem. I'm Cheyenne."

"I know."

"You know? And, how do you know my name?"

"The bartender told me last week."

"Is that so? Well, if you learned my name last week, what took you so long to use it?" I asked, failing to hide my blushing this time.

This man was the total package – sexy, charming, smelling good, beautiful teeth, dimples, sexy voice, and assertive. I just hoped he was also gay. I watched his lips as they began to move. They were a perfect size, and his teeth couldn't have been any straighter. He licked those sexy lips after every other sentence, and that caused the dimples in his cheeks to show. I continued to stare as he continued to speak. It wasn't until he asked me a question that I realized I hadn't heard a word he'd said.

"So, are you up for that?" he asked.

"Huh? Um… up for what?"

"Dinner with me tomorrow."

"Dinner?"

"Are you okay?" Hakeem asked.

"I'm sorry. Yes, I'm fine. I have a slight headache," I lied. "Dinner sounds great, but I need to tell you something before we go any further."

"Save it for dinner," he winked. "I'll see you at the steakhouse located on Line Avenue at 6:30 tomorrow evening. It was great meeting you, Cheyenne. Enjoy the rest of your night."

Before I could say another word, Hakeem had disappeared and left me speechless once again. I had a feeling of nervousness mixed with excitement forming in the pit of my stomach. So, I took a shot of tequila and said goodnight to Elisa. I needed to get my beauty rest so that I could prepare for a real date tomorrow night. I'd wait until after dinner to tell him I'm transgender so that I could at least get a meal out the deal.

As I drove home carefully trying to avoid swerving from the alcohol Elisa fed to me, my mind often drifted to Hakeem. He was gorgeous, and I couldn't wait to see him again. I thought about my outfit and what I'd do to my hair. I was excited that I could wear heels without towering over him because of his tall athletic build. I could still smell the scent of his cologne from when he shook my hand. Instead of taking a shower as I usually did after the club, I curled up in the center of my bed with my hand near my nose. I pretended that my body pillow was Hakeem and the scent of his cologne was coming from his sexy chest as I drifted off to sleep with him heavy on my mind.

CHAPTER TWO
VIVIAN

Nightmares

As I raced to the Queendom to find out how Ava could still be alive, I repeatedly replayed the evening in my head. *Bella walked up to VJ with the gun in her hand. It was aimed at him, and then she suddenly turned and shot Ava right in her head. Ava's lifeless body landed on top of her husband's corpse. She was dead just like he was. So, how could she be alive?* I mean, I know several people have survived gunshot wounds to the head, but Bella never misses. My family never misses. While I drove in a trance to the Queendom, I unconsciously picked up my phone and began to dial my mother's number. Before I could press the call button, I cleared the number and returned my phone to its position in the cupholder. I figured it would be best to review the scene before letting Bella know that her archenemy was still alive.

When I approached the mansion, I pulled around the back instead of parking in my usual spot up front and letting the guards escort me inside. Between the nightmares, my new relationship with Cheyenne, the lack of sex, and now this bullshit with Ava, I didn't feel like being bothered at all. I used my remote to open the back gates and drove through the tunnel that led to the underground entrance to the chamber. I stepped out of my black Maserati with dark tint and strutted my long legs to the door. Instead of the six-inch heels and business attire that I usually wore, I sported fitted black jeans, black combat boots, and a black hoodie. I was in no mood to deal with any issues, so I tried to be as incognito as possible.

For some reason, my heart raced as I walked down the long corridor that led to the area where the crew had moved Ava. I was afraid that Bella would flip because Ava was still potential competition. Their beef extended many years before I was even born. When Ava came to my office the first time, we made an instant connection because of her bad-ass personality and assertion. She eventually told me that she knew my mother. I didn't know the extent, and I didn't really care because business was business. I never let personal affairs get in the way of doing what I had to do. It wasn't until Ava and her husband showed up at Bella's the night of our family dinner that I learned the full details of their relationship and the beef attached to it. There was no need for me to call off our business since she was supposed to be dead. So, technically she was still my employee.

When I entered the room, Ava was in a hospital bed with machines and cords everywhere. Dawn was by her side checking her vitals. The numbers on the machine showed that her blood pressure was dangerously high. She was wearing an oxygen mask and appeared to be asleep. Her chest was heaving in and out at a rapid but steady pace. She looked like she'd age overnight. There was no way the woman lying in that bed was the same person that had assisted me with killing and torturing so many popular public officials. From superintendents to mayors to councilmen, Ava had given me the inside scoop on their activities, and we'd handled them accordingly.

"Is she alive?" I asked Dawn.

"Yes, she is. Her systolic and diastolic pressures are elevated. The bullet went through her head and exited well above the base of the skull without causing major damage. With the proper care and a bit of therapy, she could make a full recovery. She might not be as sharp as before, but she should remain within the same range of cognition."

I stood at the foot of Ava's bed and stared at her for a moment as Dawn continued to speak a bunch of medical terms about her condition. Images of the family dinner that turn into an impromptu family gathering at the Queendom popped in my mind. I thought about the pain and anger in Bella's eyes when the pillowcases were snatched from the heads of Ava and her husband. I regretted working with her from that moment forward. Regardless of my shaky relationship with my mother, I should never have worked with someone that had so much hatred for her. That thought reminded me of Cheyenne's email about the night she was raped by Deacon Rogers. I also fought back the thoughts that Ava had known about his advances for a while before he attacked her.

She knew my family and claimed to have so much respect for me; yet, she allowed her husband to harm my sister. Although she was great at doing her job for me, her hatred for my mother allowed her to ignore her husband's actions. Sure, she intervened before VJ and Marissa killed Cheyenne, but she failed to protect her from rape. I wondered if I should have ordered Dawn to give her a lethal injection and end it once and for all. Then, I thought about the amount of information Ava had on VJ's plot to kill Cheyenne. We needed the full details of his plan. Our brother would just continue to lie, and we wouldn't have another version to compare his story to if both Ava and her husband would be dead. Although VJ was in rehab, we still needed to handle him for what he did to Cheyenne. That fact alone would be reason enough to let her live, and Bella would just have to understand.

"Make sure she survives. My family's not done with her. Paul, you and the guys can stand down for now. I appreciate the phone call. Let me know if anything drastically changes," I said before exiting the room and taking the elevator to the penthouse.

I stepped off the elevator, entered the code to prevent access to the top floor, and removed my holster that held my purple 9mm Luger. I squatted down and removed the smaller handgun from my boots. I placed everything on the custom accent table that my favorite artist crafted for me. Then, I removed my combat boots. The plush carpet felt like fluffy clouds underneath my feet as I made my way to the kitchen to brew a cup of tea. As I scanned the room, I noticed my journal on the floor next to my favorite chaise lounge. With everything going on in my family, I couldn't stop thinking about Kyle. I positioned myself on the seat and emptied my thoughts on paper.

Dear Diary,

The nightmares won't go away. No matter how much time passes, I still see Kyle in my dreams. I must admit that I wasn't ready to let him go. I didn't want things to end the way they did, but he left me no choice. I'd tried so many times to get him to understand me. I expressed my needs and desires to him in hopes that we'd be on the same page in our relationship. I wanted to marry him. I'd never ever desired to be married, but something about him changed my heart and mind. Kyle loved me – at least that's what he showed me as he pursued me. He often cooked nice dinners for me followed by massages and great sex. He bought nice gifts and sent flowers to my office. He made me feel like the most beautiful girl in the world. Anything I desired, he made it happen.

Sure, I have more money than I can even count. I'm strong, smart, sexy, independent, and adventurous. However, something about Kyle just made life a little sweeter. One night, he surprised me with private swing dance lessons in our home. While we danced, a private chef created aromas that our kitchen had never experienced. Meanwhile, a saxophonist, artist, and songstress secretly waited for us poolside next to a beautiful table setting complete with fine china, a dozen long-stem roses, and an intimate paint session for two. Once the dance lessons were complete for the night, Kyle led me through our home along a thick path of rose petals to continue our beautiful evening. As our brushes stroked the canvases, the chef served our three-course meal, and we sipped wine straight from the vineyards of Napa Valley. If only we could bask in that moment for an eternity…

Our eternity came to a quick halt as soon as the saxophonist played the last note, the songstress sang the last word, and the chef served the last dish. When the *audience left, Kyle seemed to have left with them. He no longer seemed interested in our evening. He often did that. He always sent mixed signals like that. He'd be so sweet, gentle, thoughtful, and loving. Then, a switch would flip, and we'd become strangers again. He'd withdraw. It's as if he found himself falling in love, and then he'd quickly run in the other direction. After over five or more years of being together, he'd still run away when things got too sweet between us. That was Kyle. The only man I allowed behind my wall would love me like no other, and then he'd flip on me just like the guys I tried to forget from my past.*

I laid my pen down and retrieved my cup of steaming hot tea. I repeatedly tried to erase my thoughts of Kyle as the tea relaxed my body. With each nightmare, I remembered more of what happened the night he died. For years, I convinced myself that it was somehow an accident. However, I knew deep down that Queen had everything to do with his death. Lately, it's been harder and harder to control her. Usually, she only surfaced when it was time to assist a client with her issues, but now I feel her presence from the time I awaken each morning until the Ambien kicks in at night.

I've been seeing my therapist more often, and she's suggested that I find a friend to occupy my time. As far as she knows, I'm just a counselor who listens to other people's problems and then retreats to my home as a reclusive until the next day. She has no idea about my alter ego. She doesn't even know the details of my nightmares. Nonetheless, I decided to take her up on her suggestion. So, I picked up the phone and shot Tosha a message. I hadn't seen her since she came to my office and took control of me. After everything that happened in my family between VJ and Cheyenne, I figured I'd let Tosha win that one. Right now, I need to be around her. I need to open up to someone besides my therapist.

"Hey. I hope all is well. Call me when you can. I need a favor. It has nothing to do with the Queendom. Talk soon."

Before I could put my phone back down, my text alert sounded. I was surprised to see that she'd texted back so quickly.

"Hey, you! Long time no hear. I thought I ran you off. Lol What kind of favor do you need?"

"I need to see you. Let's hang out. No funny business. I just need a…"

I sent the message without finishing the last sentence. I couldn't bring myself to use that word. I didn't want to seem vulnerable.

"What do you need? A what???" she replied with eyes emoji.

"A friend, Tosha. I think I need a friend. I really don't know what I need. Can we just meet somewhere?"

I dropped my phone on the Persian rug beneath my chaise lounge and regretted even texting her. I knew it was a bad idea. As I reached for my phone to cancel my request, I received a text from her agreeing to meet me in one hour at a restaurant on the Southern Loop. My heart began to race as I went to my bedroom to change out of my war clothes into something more appropriate for brunch.

I opted for a pair of bell-bottom jeans with a few rips in the thighs and a thin long-sleeve t-shirt with a queen sporting an amazing afro on the front of it. I slipped on a pair of bedazzled Gucci slides to match my fanny pack. I fixed my hair in the mirror and applied just enough makeup to bring life to my face without overdoing it. I squirted my favorite perfume on my wrists and between my breasts. Then, I grabbed both of my guns, slipping the smaller one in my purse. I placed the holster and Luger in the safe in my closet and then headed for the elevator. I told myself I needed a friend, but it felt more like I was headed on a date.

When I arrived at the restaurant, Tosha was already seated at a table on the front patio. The fall weather was nice, so the seating was perfect. Her mouth formed an instant smile when I stepped out of the car and began to walk toward her. She stood and greeted me with a hug.

"How are you?" she asked.

"I'm well. How are you?" I replied trying to be the hard-ass that I usually portray when I'm around her.

"I was glad to receive the message from you today. I know things got a bit heated – in a good way – the last time I saw you," Tosha smiled.

I didn't respond. Instead, I kept my face as emotionless as possible while I took a seat and perused the menu. Just as Tosha cleared her throat to spark up more conversation, the waiter approached the table to take our order. I opted for charbroiled oysters and a side salad. She ordered a fried catfish po'boy with fries. As soon as the waiter left the table, I knew I would have to explain why I texted her and why I wasn't being the Vivian she's accustomed to being around. Before she could utter a word, I quickly spoke.

"I've been seeing a therapist about some personal issues that I'd rather not discuss right now. She thinks I need a friend. I'm sure you know that I don't have any friends… I'm not sure if I even know how to make any friends. So, I figured you and I could attempt to become acquaintances."

Tosha stared at me for a few seconds before she started to laugh uncontrollably. You would have thought I'd just told the funniest joke by the way she was leaned forward. She was tickled so much that her body seemed to be having convulsions. She laughed so loud and long that customers at other tables were looking in our direction. Some of them even laughed, too. Before I knew it, my stern face became a smile that turned into a laugh. After what seemed like a solid five minutes of laughter, she finally found her words.

"You are hilarious, Vivian," she said as she wiped away the tears that fell during her hysterical laughing fit.

"And, how so?" I asked as my smile began to fade.

"You've had me fooled for so long. For a moment, I felt like I was afraid of you. I know that I was definitely intimidated by you. However, the more I'm around you, the more I realize that we're no different. When you first met me, I was in a dark place with Tyrone and his bullshit. Now that I'm rejuvenated and empowered, I know that we're the same."

I sat quietly as she continued her "I'm every woman" speech.

"The last time I was in your office was the moment I knew things had shifted between us. I was slightly surprised to receive your text, but I almost expected it. What's funny is that you're still trying to play this tough role. You can't even ask for friendship without hiding the word "friend" behind its unnecessary synonym "acquaintance" for fear that you'd look weak for being human. There's nothing wrong with being human, Vivian," she said as she reached across the table and touched my hand.

Her touch was so soft and soothing. As the fall breeze inserted itself at that moment, the scent of YSL from her skin entered my nostrils and added more pleasantry. Tosha was right. I didn't want to look weak. I needed to keep the wall up so I wouldn't be hurt again. I needed to be strong for all the women who were too weak to save themselves from the pain inflicted on them by the men they loved so dearly. I didn't want someone that I once helped become a stronger woman to know that I didn't feel so strong right now. Nevertheless, I needed a friend.

"Maybe there's some truth to what you're saying, but I'm sure you understand why I must remain guarded. I've helped you through one of the toughest times of your life. How can I turn around and rely on you for anything more than business? As I said in my text, I've been seeing my therapist, and she suggested that I need a friend. I thought she was crazy at first, but she's right. So, I was thinking that you and I could hang out sometimes if that's okay with you."

"I'd like that, Vivian," she replied.

"Besides, we have some unfinished business," I said as I reached across the table and rubbed a loose strand of hair from her face.

Chapter Three
VJ

Rehabilitation

For the past couple of nights, I done woke up in a cold sweat with my heart beating out my fucking chest. Going from all access to the dope every day to getting a small portion to ween me off is fucking my body up, bruh. I need to shake back and get the fuck up out this bitch. I probably shouldn't rush that shit though because my pops is salty with a nigga about trying to kill my queer ass brother. He knows a nigga didn't mean that shit, mane. That coke be having a nigga trippin. I'm really safe from his ass while I'm in here though. I don't know what he got lined up for when a nigga gets out. I've still been plotting, but I need to chill on that shit until I find out what my family has been up to since I've been gone. The way they teamed up at the Queendom had a nigga shook. I still want what's rightfully mine, but I'll have to ease up on that for now.

"Mr. Bourdeaux, you have a visitor. Are you up for some company?" A loud voice over the PA system in my room interrupted my thoughts.

"Who is it?" I asked.

"It's your father."

This nigga must have felt me thinking about him. He's always had some kind of weird-ass psychic abilities. I contemplated pretending to be sick, but I figured he was standing close to her, ear hustling as she talked to me. I'd have to face him sooner or later, so I opted to get that shit out the way now.

"Yeah, you can send him back," I responded as I hopped up and tried to straighten up my room a little bit.

I had a few clothes bunched up in a chair and another pile in the corner by my closet. I'm usually not a junky person, but I hadn't felt like doing anything besides going home. By the time I shoved the last armful of clothes into the closet, I heard Vinny grab the knob and knock as he entered my room.

"What's up, baby?" he asked in his thick Creole accent.

"Not much, Pops. Just trying to shake back and stay out the way," I said as I walked over to greet him with a handshake.

Vinny gave my hand a squeeze and then pulled me close to him in an embrace. I was shocked to receive a hug from him, so I didn't know how to react. I gave him a pat on his back and then quickly grabbed a chair for him to have a seat. Without hesitation, he accepted my offer. He didn't waste time stating the nature of his visit.

"You know we need to discuss everything that has happened. You owe this family big time for your poor choices. I know your mother and I failed the three of you, but that's no excuse for plotting against your own flesh and blood."

Like a little boy being scolded, I dropped my head while he spoke. I didn't really feel any remorse for my actions. I just hated to face my father. His cool demeanor didn't mean he wasn't boiling with rage inside. It just meant that I needed to choose my words and actions wisely to avoid awakening the beast in that nigga. So, I chose to remain quiet while he got that shit off his mind.

He continued, "What's even worse is that you wanted someone to kill your sibling to give you a larger portion of *my* money. The money that I have shared with you so freely your whole life. The money that I was going to give each of you equally."

He sat forward in his seat with his elbows resting on his knees and his hands in the praying position in front of his mouth. He stared at me in disgust without blinking. I cut my eyes up at him and then diverted them to avoid his gaze.

"Look at your pathetic ass. You can't even be man enough to look me in the eyes and own the shit you've done. We won't finish this conversation this evening, because I can tell you're still on that shit. But I want you to know that your name has been removed from my estate so that you won't be tempted to hurt one of your siblings again. You damn sure better not fuck with your mother or me. As soon as you're released from this facility, you will right your wrongs. Do I make myself clear?"

Vinny asked as he stood to his feet and stepped closer to me.

"Yeah. I hear you," I said, trying to look him in the eyes and stop my right knee from trembling at the same time.

"Get well soon. We have a long road ahead," Vinny said as he opened the door and let himself out without another word.

I walked to the window and waited to watch him walk to the car. Moments later, he appeared on the sidewalk with his phone to his ear. I expected to see his driver pull up to get him, but he continued towards the parking lot. To my surprise, my mother pulled up in a pearl white G-wagon and swooped him up. I guess they're trying to work on their relationship. Either way, I'll never stand a chance with both of them working together. I damn sure need to bring my solid game to cancel them muthafuckas.

When their taillights were out of sight, I plopped down on my bed and laid back with one hand across my forehead and the other on my dick. Since I didn't have access to a cellphone so that I wouldn't be tempted to call my supplier to hook me up, I had to find a way to entertain myself. I grabbed the remote to the T.V. and turned to the

QVC channel. They were having a summer clearance on bathing suits. Three women were walking around modeling the swimsuits. The thick black chick had just enough ass trying to escape her bikini to get my dick hard. That's all I needed to see as I began to caress my dick until it exploded all over my hand. I got up and grabbed a dirty t-shirt from my closet to clean myself up. Then, I laid back down and drifted off to sleep. In less than two months, I'd be out this bitch and back on the streets to get what was mine.

CHAPTER FOUR
BELLA

Old Flame

Vinny asked me to drive him to visit VJ. I wasn't too keen on seeing my son right now after the mess he made of our family. Still, I wanted to spend time in Vinny's presence, so I agreed to drive him. When we pulled up to the rehab facility, he asked me to join him inside. I couldn't bring myself to get out of the car, so I sat in the parking lot while he spent a few minutes with our son. As a mother, I wanted to embrace my son during his dark time, but the boss in me wished I had put a bullet through his head for betraying our family the way he did. I turned to the smooth jazz station and laid my head back to calm my racing thoughts. I attempted the calming techniques I often taught my clients, but nothing could shake the uneasiness in the pit of my stomach. My phone began to vibrate inside my oversized checkered Louis Vuitton bag. I answered the phone without paying attention to who was calling.

"She's still alive," the voice said.

I pulled the phone from my ear to give myself a clue of what the caller could be talking about. I realized it was Vivian, but she didn't sound like herself.

"Vivian, who's alive? And, why do you sound so strange?"

"Ava. She's still alive," she slurred.

"How could that be? You all witnessed me put a bullet through her head. I never miss. Are you sure?"

"Yes, Ma. I'm sure. She's with the nurse at the Queendom. I saw her this morning with my own eyes. I didn't want to tell you because I knew you'd flip," Vivian replied with a voice full of annoyance.

"Why didn't you finish the job? I want her dead," I said calmly as I thought about all the times Ava had betrayed me.

I was reminded of the time I caught her pushing up on Vinny and how he'd restrained me so I wouldn't hang my foot up her ass on multiple occasions. That bitch was a constant problem and clearly wanted my position in my empire. I let her live too long, and I apparently fucked up the one chance I had to kill her

"That's why I'm calling, Ma. I can't kill her. I need her."

"You don't need that bitch for a muthafuckin thing!" I yelled. "Either you kill that bitch, or you deal with me finishing this shit by any means and writing you off for good."

I couldn't believe I was having to argue with my child about my orders for my empire. I'd tried my best to be a changed woman, but people insisted on bringing the old Bella back out to play. Well, if that's what they wanted, that's what they'd get. I tried that calming shit again so that I wouldn't make any rash decisions. I blew out the imaginary candles and counted down from ten. Vivian sat on the phone in silence as I counted. When I got to one, she spoke again.

"Are you good now?" I didn't reply, so she continued. "Look, Ma. I know you two have the worst relationship imaginable, but she's been a big help to my team. Plus, she has the information on VJ's plot on this family. We need to get that from her because you know he's not going to tell the truth. She also has connections that I need. I'm sorry about the pain she's caused you and this family, but I assure you that I will take full responsibility for her actions. I'll keep her out of your way and will only use her for what I need. Can you handle that?"

Rather than dignify my rebellious daughter with a response, I simply ended the call and waited for Vinny to return. It was high time that we snap our kids back into shape. They were all losing their damn minds. By the time I returned my phone to my purse, I saw my man walking through the double doors of the rehab center. I circled around to get closer and shorten his walk through the parking lot.

I loved to watch Vinny walk. It was like he was floating through the air. His white V-neck long-sleeve t-shirt hugged his chest and showed his pecks just right. He wore white fitted jeans that complimented his print, thighs, bow-legs, and his ass. Of course, he smelled good enough to eat. When I pulled around, he flashed that beautiful smile that caused his eyes to tighten. He had to be the sexiest man that God had ever created. My honey pot moistened thinking about the many nights we'd shared together over the years. Since our reconnection, I'd tried to hold off on mounting him, but I wasn't sure how much longer I could last.

"I knew you'd always be by my side," he said as he took his position in the passenger seat. "I'm gone ride with you until the wheels fall off. Is that alright with you, baby?"

"You damn right," I said as I pulled out the parking lot.

I glanced in my rearview mirror and noticed VJ staring at us from his window.

"I don't trust him," I said to Vinny.

"I don't either, mi amour. I don't either. Just know that he doesn't get another chance to fuck up."

"Speaking of fucking up... I fucked up big time. Ava didn't die. Vivian called me while you were inside with *your* son. I told her to kill the bitch, but she insists on letting her live."

"How do you feel about that?" he asked with his voice just above a whisper.

"I don't like it one bit, but she assured me that it was for business only and that she'd keep that hoe away from my family," I said as I felt anger return.

I tried the calming technique again, but I knew that bullshit wasn't going to work. The only thing that would make me feel better was if Ava was dead. Vinny could sense that my mind was drifting back to the dark side. He grabbed my hand and gave it a loving squeeze.

"Just be cool, suga mama. Don't do anything crazy. I trust that Vivian will keep her word. If shit gets out of hand, I will handle it for you. Is that cool?"

As much as I wanted to do it myself, I accepted his offer. Besides, I couldn't resist this man. He was the epitome of perfection. He rubbed my thigh as I drove back toward Shreveport. We vibed to the smooth jazz and then changed the station to Classic R&B. As if on cue, *Baby, I'm For Real (Natural High)* by After 7 bellowed through the speakers. That was my confirmation that Vinny had me like he's had me all these years. I just needed to sit back and let him drive the boat.

CHAPTER FIVE
VIVIAN

Cross the Line

A few glasses too many at lunch resulted in me calling my mother while I was in the bathroom and letting her know about Ava. It also led to Tosha driving me back to my place because I could barely see straight. She left her car at the restaurant and used my GPS to navigate us to the pin labeled "home." When we pulled up to my gated community, I told her to press the button on the remote to allow us access through the gates. We arrived at the house that I once shared with Kyle. I instructed her to park in the garage so that my nosy ass neighbors wouldn't see who was coming home with me. Once the garage door was down, we stepped out of the car and entered through the laundry room that led to the kitchen.

"Leave your shoes here and follow me," I said as I led her down the long hallway to my master bedroom. She didn't say much as she followed my orders. When we got to my room, I pressed the button on the light switch that turned the lights down low. Then, I connected my phone to the Bluetooth surround sound system and scrolled to John Legend's *Cross the Line*. I grabbed Tosha by the hand and began to dance with her slowly and sensually as John sang my thoughts.

"Only just a friend.
The love story begins.
Now here's a happy ending to believe in.
And always there for me.
Now you're with me in my dreams
It's got me wondering if you ever
Dream of me.
I don't want to risk losing everything
But I'll take a chance and tell you what I'm thinking.

Girl, you'll be my best friend,
Can we put this to bed then?
Tonight's the night

To cross the line
Baby, won't you be mine?
Not just my homegirl
Time that I take you home girl
Tonight's the night
To cross the line
Let me love you tonight."

While he sang, we danced, kissed, and rubbed all over each other. No one was in control. We were both lost in the moment that we'd danced around for so long. At home, I wasn't Viv or Queen. I was Vivian, the human being that needed this moment with her. I needed to be loved, touched, rubbed, and tasted. I needed to do the same to her… with her… for her. We needed so much, and we gave each other just that.

Kiss, kiss, kiss me on my lips
We've been dancing 'round the moment
Now we're doing it.
Breathe, breathe
And sigh your sweet relief
We've been holding it so long,
The wait was killing me
Oh, and we are what we have been waiting for.

I slowly walked her to my bed and pulled the canopy closed on each side. I wanted us to be the only two people in the world at that moment. She laid back and allowed me to kiss her lips, nibble her earlobes, and run my tongue around each nipple. While my tongue tasted her sweet skin, my fingers slipped inside her dripping pussy. I rubbed her clit vigorously and then tasted my fingers. I transferred her taste from my lips to her mouth as I kissed her so passionately. I love men and dick dearly, but it was something about the sensuality of being with a woman that drove me wild. She smelled good and tasted even better.

I undressed myself to match her nakedness. Before I could resume the consumption of her body, she flipped me over and took charge. Instead of the sensual gestures I used on her, she forcefully grabbed my legs behind each knee and stretched them open and up toward my head. Then, she shoved her face inside my pussy and devoured me until I squirted on her tongue. I was ready to tap out, but she had some shit to get off her chest. Before I could make another move, she straddled me and rubbed our clits together like a pro. It was a feeling that I'd never felt before, but I knew I didn't want it to end. Once again, Tosha was in control. After what seemed like an eternity, we joined each other in a squirting contest and then she collapsed beside me.

"That was beyond words," she said between gasps for air.

I got up and grabbed us both a warm towel from the bathroom before returning to the bed and cleaning the sex from her body and then mine.

"Would you like something to drink?" I asked as I leaned down and grabbed a bottle of water from the mini-fridge.

"Water would be great," she said, sounding as if she'd finally caught her breath.

I tossed her the bottle and turned the music down low to allow us the opportunity to talk. I was open at that moment so she could ask me anything she needed to know. We laid in silence for a few minutes and savored what had just happened. Finally, she spoke.

"So, what now?"

"You tell me," I replied.

"You still need that friend?"

"Yeah, if you'll accept my offer."

"Offer? To work for you?" she asked seemingly annoyed.

"No, I wasn't even thinking about that. Although, that wouldn't be a bad idea. But I was talking about my offer of the friendship that my therapist suggested."

She leaned over and kissed my lips.

"Sure, if I can get one of these sessions every now and then.

"I don't think I can handle you," I joked. "You seem to be more advanced than I expected."

"I told you Tyrone had me doing all kinds of shit to keep him pleased, and then he still chose to fuck around on me. What's even worse is that one of his bitches has a dick."

I'd almost forgotten about Cheyenne's relationship with Tosha's husband. I figured this would be a great time to let her know she was my sister.

"Had," I said.

"Had? What are you talking about?"

"Cheyenne had a dick, but she doesn't anymore."

She sat up in the bed and prepared to stand.

"I knew you'd been working with his whores. You seem to know a lot about them. Is that why you wanted me here, Vivian? Is this some kind of sick joke? You know what that shit did to me! How could you play me like this?"

She began to redress quickly as she yelled at me.

"Tosha! Would you give me a second to respond!?"

Her attitude was awakening Viv who would soon become Queen if she wasn't careful. Maybe my eyes or heavy breathing sent the message of my thoughts because she suddenly stopped yelling and took a seat on my footstool.

"Cheyenne is my transgender sister. I had no idea who she was until a year or so later. I never thought about her whenever I saw you. You can attest that our moments together have always been too intense for words or thoughts. It just dawned on me when you mentioned your husband again. I was too caught up in my own issues, and I was trying to focus and keep myself in order. This is why I have not allowed anyone close to me. I need you to know that I would never play games with you like this," I said as I took a seat next to her on the stool. "I've been battling my own demons and haven't had time to think about anything or anyone else. I lowered the music to give us a chance to talk. Ask me anything you'd like to know."

"Are you being honest with me?"

"Yes, I am," I replied.

"That's all I need for now. Take me to my car, please. We can revisit this conversation later. I enjoyed this time with you… friend," she said before heading to the car. I smiled slyly and followed her.

CHAPTER SIX
CHEYENNE

New Love

The sun beamed through my bedroom window bright and early Friday morning. I woke up feeling refreshed and energetic, so I decided to clear my schedule and flow with the wind that day. I rolled out of bed and freshened up before going to the kitchen to juice the fruit I bought from the Farmer's Market last week. I made a variation of mango-strawberry-kiwi, watermelon-orange-apple, mango-peach-strawberry, and any other combination I could create from the beautiful fruits on the countertop. As I was cleaning up the kitchen, the text alert on my phone sounded. I dried my hands on the decorative towel and grabbed the phone to see who was messaging me at 7:00 a.m. I was shocked and a bit flattered to see that I was on Hakeem's mind this early in the morning.

I opened the message and immediately blushed at the cutest bitmoji waving at me. I was expecting to see an unsolicited dick pic that men typically volunteered to show off their morning wood. I was also prepared to clown his ass and kick him to the curb as quickly as he forced his way into my life.

Instead of having to curse him, I sent a flirtatious emoji back. Then, I went to his social media page and liked a picture that was deep in his images. He sent a kissing emoji and then returned the social media like. We played this flirting game without words for about five minutes before he sent the first words.

> *"Brunch?"*
> *"I thought you said dinner…"*
> *"I can't wait that long to see you."*

He was still laying the charm on thickly. I blushed and then replied.

"Sure… Where?"
"Any preferences?" he asked.
"Not really… Somewhere pretty with great food…"
"I know a place… May I pick you up?"

I hesitated before responding to his last question. I was skeptical about letting new guys know where I lived. After Tyrone and his lies, I needed to be careful. I almost agreed, but something in the pit of my stomach told me to decline his offer.

"Not yet," I said.
"I understand. No worries. Meet me at Chef George's Bistro. He makes the best Shrimp 'N Grits you'll ever taste."
"Awesome! See you in thirty," I said as I rushed to freshen up and find the right jeans to fit my voluptuous curves.

When I arrived at Chef George's, Hakeem was standing near the entrance waving at me. I quickly met him, and we walked in together.

"Were you waiting long?" I asked as he held up two fingers to the hostess to indicate that we needed a table for two.

"Nah… no more than a couple of minutes. I poked my head inside to see if you had already made it. I'd just stepped back outside when you pulled up."

A gust of wind from the door opening blew the scent of his cologne through my nostrils down to my soul. I could have melted right there in the foyer of the bistro, but I caught myself. A young, bubbly waitress with 3A hair pulled back into a curly afro puff led us to our table.

"My name is Alexis, and I'll be taking care of you this morning. May I start you off with anything to drink or an appetizer?"

"What are the options?" Hakeem asked.

"Our brunch menu is available from 7 a.m. to 1 p.m. We have endless mimosas or poinsettias for $10. We also have fruit juices that come with the buffet."

"I'll take a Grapefruit Mimosa," I chimed in.

"I'll have the same," Hakeem added.

"No problem. I'll bring a pitcher to your table. You may help yourself to the brunch buffet,"

Alexis said as she pointed to the array of food that was set up buffet style.

"Thanks so much," I said as I prepared to stand and head to the buffet.

Hakeem grabbed my hand and stopped me from moving.

"Let's talk for a sec unless you're going to pass out from hunger."

I giggled from embarrassment and returned to my seat.

"I think I'll manage," I laughed. "What's on your mind?"

"You."

"What about me?"

"Everything. I want to get to know you better," he said as he grazed my hand with his fingertips.

"What do you want to know?" I asked.

I began to feel nervous because I knew the topic of my sexuality would arise sooner or later. This was always a touchy subject for me because straight men tend to let their egos and testosterone lead to violence against transgender women. I only agreed to go on this date with him because of the rumors I'd heard about him.

"For starters, I've asked around about you and couldn't believe what I've heard. So, I wanted to ask you myself. Are you –"

"Yes! I'm transgender!" I blurted before he could finish.

By then, Alexis had returned with our drinks. She quickly placed our mimosas on the table and excused herself without asking if we needed anything else. I take it that she caught a glimpse of our conversation.

"Transgender?" he replied. "That's nice to know, but I was asking if you were single. I didn't think a woman as beautiful as you are could really be single, but thanks for the additional information."

Anyone could have bought me for a penny at that moment. I wanted to literally slide down in my seat and find refuge underneath that table. I had no words, so I guzzled the first mimosa that was already in the glass Alexis had placed on the table and then grabbed the pitcher to pour myself another one.

"Thirsty?" he asked.

"Embarrassed," I replied between gulps like I was in a mimosa marathon.

"Why are you embarrassed? Don't you think I already knew that?" he asked as he placed a soft finger under my chin and lifted my head up to meet his eyes. "Stop being hard on yourself. I can't say that I know what you've gone through, but I can say that I've received so much scrutiny for being attracted to women like you."

I breathed a sigh of relief when I realized that I didn't have a secret at all. Then, I let out a silent belch from the champagne bubbles that had formed in my belly. I wanted to delve deeper into that conversation but opted to visit the buffet instead. If things continued to progress this way between us, Hakeem and I would have plenty of time to talk. I stood, grabbed him by the hand, and led him to the buffet. Then, I handed him a plate and took one for myself. We didn't mention anything else about sexuality. We just piled our plates with amazing food and enjoyed each other's company for the next couple of hours.

Chapter Seven
Vinny

Family Meeting

My family is in a bittersweet state right now. I have a great relationship with Vivian and Charley, even though he's living his life as a woman. What's even better is that I finally have the love of my life back, and I'm never letting her go. Bella has been the best thing to ever happen to me. I've never met a woman so strong and powerful yet so sweet and simplistic. I didn't do right by her when we were together over twenty years ago. I was a young hothead with more money than I could count and more women than I could manage. When I brought Bella in off the streets, I had every intention to live up to my promise of giving her a better life. But, like the typical young rich nigga, I fucked over her and watched her life crumble before my eyes. I could have saved her, but I chose the streets. Now that I have her back, I will do everything in my power to fulfill those promises and more.

Unfortunately, I will never be able to trust VJ again. My namesake had the audacity to attempt the ultimate betrayal of my kingdom. He has lost this family's trust, and he will never get it back. He hasn't felt my wrath yet, but it's coming. I just need to calculate my steps a few moves ahead like chess since he knows how I operate. Naturally, I taught my boy everything about the business and how to take down the enemy. What I didn't realize is that I was training him to try to take down his brother and possibly overthrow me. I held nothing back from VJ because I needed my empire to continue to flourish if anything ever happened to me. Now, I regret being so open with him, but I will get my revenge.

As I sat on the pier of Bella Terrace, Ernest announced my family's arrival.

"Mr. Bourdeaux, here's Ms. Bella, Ms. Vivian, and Ms. Cheyenne. Appetizers will be served shortly," he said as he returned to the outdoor kitchen to retrieve the appetizers.

Bella was looking beautiful as usual. I stood to greet her first by placing a soft kiss on her lips. She returned the kiss and ended it with a nibble on my lips.

"Get a room!" my children said simultaneously before high-fiving each other and sharing laughter.

"Don't hate," Bella said as she licked her tongue out and took a seat in the chair closest to mine.

I walked over and greeted Vivian and Cheyenne both with a hug and peck on the cheek. I wasn't fully comfortable with Charley's transition, but family is important. So, I was learning to accept my child regardless. Each of them grabbed an empty chair and waited for me to speak.

"I'm sure you all know why we're here. I'll cut the bullshit. VJ will be home soon. In light of everything that has transpired, you must know that I do not trust him. Personally, I'd love to kill that little muthafucka, but your mother here has requested that I let him live," I said as I looked over at my beautiful woman before continuing. "I have beefed up security and added a bodyguard to watch his every move. Since I can't get rid of him, I need to keep him close and within arm's length. Cheyenne, I don't want you alone with him. In the event something happens to me, I need you all to know that VJ is forbidden to receive anything from my estate. I've completed the paperwork with my attorney to remove his name from everything. Bella gets half, and you two get twenty-five percent apiece. If you kill me, you get nothing," I said.

"I'll try to keep you alive," Bella said as she rubbed my leg underneath the table.

"If you don't keep your hands to yourself, you might kill the old man right now," Vivian added and threw in a fake gag.

Cheyenne didn't say much. She just sat quietly and smiled.

"Is everything okay?" I asked.

"Yeah. I'm fine. I'm just nervous about him getting out. I mean, what if he tries it again?"

"Listen to me," I said sternly and leaned forward. "If you think I will let some shit like that happen again, you must be crazier than your fuckin brother. I will personally fuck him up if he even blinks wrong. This is MY family! I will not let anything happen to any of you! Do I make myself clear?" I asked as I made eye contact with each of them.

"We understand, babe," Bella added.

"We know you're crazy," Vivian said to lighten the mood. "You and Ma taught me everything I know."

We all laughed, but a stillness filled the air. I couldn't let my family walk around in paranoia. I needed revenge on my son for the pain he caused this family. I'd try to honor Bella's wishes, but I was itching to snap his neck for the least offense.

"After we've finished our meal, I'd like each of you to join me at my private shooting range. I know we've practiced so many times before, but it's been a while and I need to know that you're ready for war. Did you bring your weapons with you?"

"Of course," they all said as they reached in their purses and then placed their pieces on the table.

"Very good. Very good. I like that. I need you to stay ready. I haven't been able to rest. I feel like something is about to happen," I said as I took a sip of my drink.

Bella leaned back in her seat and stared in the distance before speaking.

"Vivian, I told your father about Ava being alive. I hope you have her under control. If she fucks with my family again, I will dismantle her body and ship that shit to her nearest relative. When your father can't sleep, that's usually a solid sign that some shit is about to go down. Keep a close eye on her. If she moves wrong, lock her up and then let me do the honors of assuring her death."

"You have my word," Vivian said while holding her mother's hand and staring in her eyes for certainty.

"Wait? She's alive?" Cheyenne chimed in.

"Yeah. I'll fill you in later," Vivian said.

"No need. Just let me kill her since it's my fault that all of this has happened," Cheyenne chimed in.

"Baby, this is not your fault," Bella said quickly. "Your brother is sick and jealous, and he linked up with the evilest slut to fulfill his greed. That had nothing at all to do with you."

Cheyenne didn't respond verbally, but a look of vengeance filled her eyes as if they were the window to her dark soul. I didn't know what she was thinking, but I could see that she was truly a Bourdeaux that was ready for war.

"Grab your weapons. We'll train with them in addition to the artillery in the range. Let's get ready for war," I said as I stood and led my family down the cobblestone path to my private shooting range.

CHAPTER EIGHT
BELLA

This Is MY Family!

Bella from the Block has been brewing inside me since Cheyenne's attack. I've repeatedly tried to suppress her, but her rage is eating me alive and begging to be reborn. Ava should be dead. When Vivian learned that she was still alive, she should have killed her with no question. Instead, her selfishness and desire to be in control took over as usual. Now, I'm forced to bring back the old me. Bella of the past was a tough broad that would pop a muthafucka in a heartbeat and sleep peacefully at night. Vinny had turned me into a person that was far worse than who I was when I moved to Shreveport. He developed a person within me that was even a stranger to myself. Still, I let her take over my life.

That dark soul existed for many years until I found myself inside a confessional one afternoon pouring out my darkest secrets to the priest. I needed to rid my heart and mind of my actions and restart my life as a better person. So, I stepped away from the streets and developed a support group for battered women. I hated the person that I had been for so many years, and I needed to find a better way to help women. I needed to get right with God. That also meant cutting ties with anything and anyone associated with my past. Vinny had already kicked me out and took my sons. I was raising Vivian the best I could, but Ava was always around to remind me of what I used to be. She'd always been jealous of me, even on my worst days. She had a couple of sons over the years, but I never got the chance to meet them. I eventually ended our friendship and went on with my life.

When I learned that Vivian lived an alternate lifestyle, I tried to talk some sense into her. However, like the old me, she wouldn't listen. She craved revenge and would do anything to fulfill her desires. While it was shocking that she and Ava had been working together, I wasn't surprised because each of us has shared desires. Regardless, Ava must die. If Vivian can't bring herself to kill her, I'll do it myself. This is my family, and I refuse to allow my son, my archenemy, or anyone else to control us. The Lord would have to forgive me for backsliding to help my family. Vinny's getting up in age, Vivian's been off lately, and Cheyenne is too weak for this lifestyle, I thought as I walked into my bathroom and turned on a steamy shower.

Before I could undress, my cell began to ring on the counter. I was surprised to see the name of VJ's rehab facility calling. I specifically told them to only call me if there was a dire emergency. Other than that, call his father or deal with it themselves.

"This is Bella," I answered in an agitated tone.

"What's up, Ma? This is VJ. How you been?"

"I've been fine. What do you want?"

"Damn, Ma. Why you gotta be so short with a nigga? I know I fucked up, but I'm dealing with all that shit right now. On god, it won't happen again. I'm not fucking with no drugs or none of that shit no more, man."

As VJ pleaded his case to me, I felt myself growing more furious. I hated the sound of his voice. I hated the lame ass game he tried to run on me all the time. I allowed that shit for years because I knew Vinny had fucked him up. But, to know that he would stoop low enough to attempt to murder his sibling removed any loving feelings I had for my son. I tried to be cordial just as I promised Vinny.

"I don't mean to be short, son. I was in the middle of doing something, and your call caught me off guard," I lied. "How are you? When do they plan to release you?"

"I'm good. Taking it one day at a time. They said I'm progressing quickly and might get an early release. Have you checked on my place and made sure it's still standing?"

"Your father has been handling that. He goes by your place weekly. Listen, I don't mean to rush you off the phone, but I really need to finish what I'm doing. I'm glad you're okay. Thanks for calling," I said before quickly hanging up.

Nothing in VJ's tone said he was a changed man. He still sounded vindictive and manipulative. The only benefit of that call was learning that he'd be home sooner than we expected. I needed to alert my family and prepare them for whatever bullshit he might bring home with him. Before I could dial Vinny's number to inform him of the call, Cheyenne's name appeared on my screen as an incoming call.

"What's up, Charl- I mean Cheyenne?"

"I need you to teach me the game," she said without even acknowledging the name slip-up.

"What game, baby?" I asked, knowing exactly what she meant. I just needed to hear the words myself.

"The gangsta life. My dad has always talked about how bad you used to be and how much he learned from you. He told me that you helped him a lot back in the day and that you saved his life on several occasions. You know he shunned me because of the sugar in my tank, so I never got to learn the streets like VJ did. I know a little bit from eavesdropping, but I don't think I know the game well enough to protect myself from VJ or anyone else who might try to attack me. I saw how great of shot you were at the range. Teach me what you know."

I listened as my child rambled nervously and begged for my help. I didn't like the idea of possibly training one of my children to kill the other, but I also needed her to be ready if we had to go to war.

"Say no more. I'll teach you the game if you promise to keep our lessons a secret."

"That's not a problem."

"Don't even tell Vivian," I said sternly.

"You have my word… but, what's up with you two? I could tell something was off the other day. Did I miss anything?"

"I'm just not keen on the fact that she has allowed Ava to live after all that she's done to this family. Now, I'm forced to return to a lifestyle that I thought I'd never see again."

"Don't worry, Ma. Teach me the game and trust that I will always have your back no matter what."

"Deal," I said before ending the call.

I finished undressing and took a long hot shower to wipe away the stress of the past few months. I needed my head to be clear for whatever was about to happen next. Rather than contacting

Vinny to spend the night with him. I finished my shower and lit every candle I could find. I placed them in a circle in the middle of my bedroom floor. Then, I sat in the middle of the circle of candles and folded my legs with my feet resting on each of my thighs and my arms extended. My index fingers and thumbs created a small circle on each hand. I closed my eyes and inhaled peace while releasing pain and anger. I continued this meditation procedure until I felt relaxed and mentally clear. After that, I blew out the candles, rolled a nice sized joint, climbed into my king-size bed, and puffed until I fell asleep. The Bourdeaux Family war was quickly approaching, and I needed to be ready.

CHAPTER NINE
VJ

I'm Coming Home

"What's up, Tyrone? This is ya boy VJ. How's everything looking out there?"

"What's going on, man? Shit's wild as fuck right now. My moms didn't die. She's chillin at your sister's place where they fucked me up at."

"Word?! How you know?" I asked, shocked as shit to hear that.

"Ava called me one day from an unknown number. At first, I didn't know who she was because she sounded bad and shit. Then, I thought someone could have been playing on my phone. She ended up telling me some shit that only you and I know, and that confirmed it for me," Tyrone said.

"What she say nigga? And, how do you know she was alone?" I asked.

I didn't trust this nigga one bit, but I knew I could use him on my team since he hated Vivian as much as I do. He's been separated from his wife, Tosha, since he got caught up in a fucked up situation fucking around with Marissa and Cheyenne. I had gotten Marissa on my side to plot against Cheyenne. Then, that muthafucka got scared and confessed and shit. I remembered seeing his number in Marissa's phone one night after we got fucked up and she told me all about how that shit went down with them. So, I stole the number and reached out to the nigga to get revenge on them. I knew he was salty enough to do it. At first, he was skeptical, but when I mentioned the amount of money that we'd both end up with, he was in there like swimwear.

He told me the story of him dressing up as a woman and going to see my sister, Vivian. I knew then that I could get him to do damn near anything. The more I talked to the nigga, I found out that he was the son to Ava and her husband. He had a fraternal twin brother named Kyle who disappeared mysteriously. That's also the nigga that Vivian was crazy about. They think she had something to do with his disappearance, which is why Ava wants to stick so close to her. Tyrone had never met Vivian before the day he visited her office because Kyle was always secretive about his love life. Plus, Tyrone lived in Chicago and only came to Shreveport for work. If they linked up, it would be at a bar for a few drinks.

Ava hipped him to who she was. After his visit, the ladies assumed it was only to find out more about her services and what she taught women. What they didn't know was that he wanted to avenge his brother's death. It also turns out that Ava used to run the streets with my moms back in the day. In other words, our families are connected in all kinds of fucked up ways. Tyrone also hates his parents for forcing him and his brother to grow up too fast. They grew up afraid of their parents, and this nigga didn't get the love he wanted as a child. So, he's on some mommy and daddy issues type shit. Nonetheless, we want the same thing in the end, so we're working together to get paid. We just need to get Tosha onboard with our plan.

"She mentioned Kyle and your sister's relationship. She also mentioned the real reason I went to see Vivian that day at her office. That was always our code before we discussed our plans. She's still down with getting rid of your family, and I'm still down of blowing her fucking brains out when the job is done. Anyway, when you getting out of there? We need to get this ball rolling before anyone finds out my mom is still alive," Tyrone said.

"They're thinking about giving me an early release since I'm shaking back so quickly in a short time. I have to stay at least two more weeks to meet the minimum requirement of two months though. You think you can hold it down until then?" I asked.

"Bet," he replied.

"Aight, bruh. Try to reach out to Tosha to see if she's still down for ya. We need to use her to our advantage. Slide her some dick or something," I laughed.

"Oh, one more thing. My mom had my cousin working on Cheyenne before you got my dad involved and all that shit went down. Now that he's dead, we need to make sure Hakeem can hold his own and keep an eye on ya girl. I need everyone occupied so they won't team up on us like last time."

"My nigga, you are brilliant. Let's do this shit!" I exclaimed.

"Hit me back in a couple of days, and I'll let you know how it plays out. Holla," Tyrone said before ending the call.

I could taste the blood and money that would be mine. Ava wanted revenge on Bella for taking my pops, so she could handle them. I hated Vivian just because she thought she knew everything and could get money better than I could. Charley's a fucking queer so that's enough already. Tyrone knew his mom loved his brother more than she loved him. I didn't give a fuck about that kind of shit, but if that's what fueled that nigga's rage, I'd use it to my advantage. I'd get that nigga to do all this work and then pop his ass once he cashed out the money his mom would leave him. Hakeem would just have to be a casualty.

CHAPTER TEN
AVA

A Mother's Love

After being locked away at the Queendom for what seems like years, I needed to find a way to get out and back to my life. The great news was that Vivian had decided to let me live. However, I had no idea what her plans were for me. I damn sure didn't plan to stick around for her to torture me like she did my son, nor would I let her kill me like she did my sweet Kyle. I needed to figure a way to butter up her guards or to get her wrapped around my finger again. As I laid in bed thinking of a way to get myself back into the world and away from Vivian's control, the nurse came in to dope me up with more medicine.

"It's time for your afternoon meds, Ava," Nurse Dawn said with a smile.

She was a sweet girl and didn't seem like the type of person that would work for Vivian. I wondered where she found her. Most importantly, I wondered if I could use her to get myself out of here.

"Oh, sweetheart, I'm feeling great today. Must I take those meds again?" I asked in the sweetest old lady voice that I could muster up.

"Of course, you do, Mrs. Ava. We have to make sure there's no infection building up inside your brain. You were almost dead. We want to be sure that your brain is functioning well enough to be relea… I mean, well enough for Vivian to give us the next steps."

She knew that I'd never be released from this hell hole, which is why she caught herself before finishing that word. She knew that Vivian would hold me here, nurse me back to health, and then play fucked up mind games to control me like she's done so many other people. I knew her game though. She played it just like her mother. They reeled people in and enticed them before playing them like pawns. Bella thinks she won because she ended up with Vinny. I surrendered back then, but I never forgave her for taking him from me. That could have been me in that nice ass mansion on forty acres of land with that sexy ass Creole kingpin. I taught her the ropes before she met him and then she added her charm and took the man that I had been wanting for years.

To make matters worse, Vivian took my Kyle away from me and then killed him. He would always talk about this woman he worked with and how much he loved her. I was excited for him until I saw her picture and immediately noticed her resemblance to Bella. I asked him if he knew her mother's name. When he confirmed it, I forbade him to see her again. It was too late because he had already fallen in love with her and had plans to marry her. He eventually grew tired of me threatening to cut him out of my will if he continued to see her. As a result, he moved without telling me where he lived. He wouldn't even let Tyrone come to his house for fear that he'd tell me the address. He'd answer my calls, but that suddenly stopped. When I saw the news story of his company burning and a body being found amid the ashes, I knew it had to be my Kyle and that bitch Vivian had everything to do with it.

Through the proper connections, I found out where her main office was and went to her with a sob story about my husband being attracted to transgender women. We had an instant connection, and I began to work for her. She trusted me, which gave me access to Marissa who would eventually begin dating VJ after it didn't work out between her and my Tyrone. I knew that I could get Marissa to work with me since she was so hurt by losing Tyrone to his wife and having to compete against her closest friend, Cheyenne, for a man. My plan was coming together until my sick ass husband raped Cheyenne and caused her to get her family involved. I knew that I needed to kill him, but I couldn't face the Bourdeaux family alone. So, I enlisted the help of VJ, Tyrone, and Tosha.

VJ was easy, considering his drug habit and thirst for their family fortune. Tyrone was a no-brainer because he longed to be my special boy like Kyle had been since they were born. He would do anything to be the twinkle of my eye. Tosha... Tosha was a problem. She's still a problem. Vivian has her under her spell, and nothing can break that. She used to be blindly in love with Tyrone even after all his cheating, STDs, and possible outside children. That was until she came across Vivian McQueen. I have no idea what she did to Tosha, but I know it has had her in a trance since she finally agreed to meet with her.

Even after Tosha and my son decided to divorce, she was still in contact with me. I had her on my side. I convinced her that she needed revenge and that I could help her heal. I told her that I knew about Vivian's proposition, but I could make her a better offer and she'd get my son back. She was all in. I'd gotten her to start avoiding Vivian's calls and cancelling meetings with her. I was going to have her do whatever I needed done. Then, she called me crying one day saying she couldn't hurt Vivian or anyone else. I didn't know what could have changed her mind. But she kept talking… She revealed that she had romantic feelings for Vivian, and she couldn't hurt another person she loved. She no longer wanted to be with Tyrone. She wanted Vivian. Vivian had won again.

I tried to pretend that I understood how she felt, but I was fuming inside. I backed off for a while to give her time to calm down, but I knew I needed another plan. As if Satan himself had heard my unspoken thoughts, my nephew Hakeem's name was in a headline on the breaking news. He'd been dropped by the NBA for multiple injuries. That was my chance to offer him the same money he was making if he would come work for me. I'd always suspected him of being gay when he was growing up, so I used that as my ammunition. Before my husband got us wrapped up in a war zone with the Bourdeaux family, I called him over to comfort him during such a lifechanging experience. Prior to his arrival, I had pictures of women laying around as if I was choosing them for a pageant. I included a picture of Cheyenne that I'd stolen from her social media page. He pretended to be interested in the women as he thumbed through the photos and made sexual comments about them. It wasn't until he reached Cheyenne's photo that I saw his eyes truly light up. I knew I had him, and my plan would fall right into place.

"Who is this?" he asked, trying to seem uninterested.

"Oh, that's a nice young lady, but she might not be your type."

"Why do you say that?"

"As beautiful as she is, she wasn't born a woman," I said as I glanced over the top of my eyeglasses to see his reaction.

He shifted in his seat and cleared his throat before speaking.

"Oh wow. I would never have known. Good looking out, auntie," Hakeem said as he placed the picture of Cheyenne back on the table.

He gave her another quick glance before turning back towards me.

"I could arrange a meeting if you'd like. You don't have to hide anything from your Auntie Ava. I've always known, suga," I said as I stood next to him with my arm draped across his shoulders. "I heard the rumors, but I wasn't going to mention it to you until you were ready to tell me yourself. Your auntie has done her share of shit, so I can't utter a word about you."

"I appreciate that," he said as if a burden had been lifted off his shoulders.

The sincerity and innocence in his eyes almost made me rethink my plan, but the devil in me couldn't resist the moment of vulnerability.

"I just need a small favor from you," I said as I grabbed a seat directly across from him.

I needed to see his eyes to determine how far I'd go with my request. He sat up straight in his seat like he always did when he meant business.

We'd always had a great relationship, so I knew he'd trust me.

"Once you get to know her, I need you to find out anything you can about her family. We're in the same line of business, and I need to know their every move so that I can remain a few steps ahead of them. I'll pay you for any information you can bring me on them."

"I gotcha, auntie. Now, what's her name and how do I find her?"

I smiled at how easy it was to get Hakeem to agree to my plan.

"Her name is Cheyenne, and she hangs out at Metropolis on Thursdays."

"Say no more," he said as he stood and kissed me on the cheek before leaving.

That was a few months ago, and everything was flowing smoothly in no time. He'd started frequenting the club to see if Cheyenne would be there. Before he could make his move, he informed me that she'd disappeared. That also happened to be during the time my husband decided to rape her and bring havoc into our lives. I hadn't spoken with him since our initial meeting. Tyrone is the only person who even knows I'm still alive besides Vivian and her crew. I managed to sneak a call in to him when the nurse left her phone on my bed and stepped out of the room while I pretended to be sleep. It was nice to know that my son was still in touch with VJ. I also asked him to check on Hakeem and find a way to get me out of the chamber even if that meant killing everyone that got in his way.

CHAPTER ELEVEN
CHEYENNE

Something Just Ain't Right

"It's so good lovin' somebody and somebody loves you back. To be loved and love in return is the only thing that my heart desires," Teddy Pendergrass's vocals rang through my car's speakers and I sung off-key as I pulled into Hakeem's driveway. Things had been going well between us. If we didn't see each other every day, it was at least every other day. It was as if he couldn't get enough of me just like I couldn't get enough of him. For the first time since

my transition, I was in what felt like a real relationship. I was free to be myself without being judged or asked a bunch of weird or uncomfortable questions. I didn't want to jinx it, but I could see myself falling in love with Hakeem.

Before I could ring the doorbell to his multi-million dollar mansion, he was answering the door in silk boxers, an apron, and a chef's hat that read: Kiss the Chef. I leaned in and met his lips.

"Someone missed me," he said as he stepped aside and allowed me to enter his home. "Did you have a hard time getting through the gates? I was waiting for you to call me and then I heard your music blaring when you pulled up."

"It wasn't blaring," I said as I playfully smacked him on the butt while following him to the kitchen. "No, I followed another car through the gates with no issues. The food smells great. What are you cooking? I already know what's on the menu for dessert."

He blushed and made his pecks jump before replying, "I love the parmesan crusted chicken they make at the steakhouse. Since we've been going out so much, I thought I'd cook this for you instead. I know you love the beef, so I'm also searing a couple of steaks," he said with a wink.

I glanced down at the rising bulge in his pants and made the slurping sound with my mouth before grabbing the bottle of wine and reading the label. We hadn't been intimate yet, but things got very heated during a make out session. We agreed to wait ninety days before having sex because we know how it can complicate things. We limited our interactions to flirting and kissing only.

"I got that when I visited an Italian vineyard last year. I wanted to save it for the perfect occasion. Feel free to open it and pour us a couple of glasses. The electric wine opener should be in that drawer next to the fridge."

I blushed at his statement and then made my way over to the drawer. As I thumbed through the contents, I noticed a slip of paper with my family's names listed on it. My heart began to beat out of my chest as I turned to confront him. As if he knew what I'd seen, he quickly began to speak.

"It's not what you think," he said nervously.

"Just what the hell is this!? Have you been plotting on me this whole time muthafucka?" I asked as I reached for the knife that he'd been using to chop up the veggies.

"Plotting? No! Of course not! It was a gift. I was going to surprise you with something that included your family's names. You talked about them so much that I wanted to do something nice for you," he said without taking his eyes off the knife.

"I've been through enough shit, Hakeem. I can't take another heartbreak. Are you being straight with me?" I asked without loosening my grip on the knife that was pointed at his throat.

"Chey, baby, I'd never do anything to hurt you. I'm finally free to love, and I refuse to fuck that up. Look, I'll show you what I've been working on. O-open up… open up that pantry door and look to the left. I was going to surprise you after dinner," he stuttered.

I walked backwards toward the door and kept my eyes locked on him. When I opened the door, I was greeted by a beautiful painting of the Bourdeaux family tree. My eyes filled with tears as I placed the knife on the counter and gave Hakeem the tightest apology hug ever.

"I'm sorry, babe. I've just been so paranoid after everything that's happened to me. My hormones are still adjusting, and I tend to have labile episodes sometimes. Please forgive me."

I could feel his heart pounding when I hugged him. I felt so horrible and hoped I didn't ruin our evening.

"It's cool, but I'm going to need something stronger than this wine after that shit," he laughed. Pull that henny out the freezer and pour us a couple of shots. There should be two shot glasses right next to the bottle. Then, you sit your ass waaayy over there and enjoy that painting," he said as he continued to whip up dinner.

"Thanks, by the way. This is the nicest thing anyone has ever done for me. I really appreciate you, and I apologize again for my reaction," I said feeling so embarrassed but still a bit skeptical.

"Nah, it's cool. I probably would have done the same thing if my new boo had my family lineage tucked away in a drawer."

"Boo? I thought we were just chillin," I flirted.

"Yeah, I'm chillin with my, boo. I ain't doing all this cooking for nothing. You belong to me now," he said as he licked his lips and flashed that sexy smile that captured me the first night that I saw him in the club.

Something wasn't right in my spirit, but I'd cross that bridge when I got to it. In the meantime, I would enjoy being free with this six-foot-nine hunk of a man in front of me.

"Alright then, boo. You mind if I turn on some music?"

"Be my guest. The Bluetooth is already on; just connect to Mr. Blackshire's Beats on the list."

I found his name on the list and connected my phone. Then, I went to the playlist that I was bumping when I pulled into his yard. *Sex is On My Mind* by Bluelight was next on the list. I tried to skip past it, but Hakeem insisted that I let it play. He sang the song, fucking up a few words along the way as he finished cooking. I learned more about his family and was sad to hear that his parents died in a freak accident. He was raised by his aunt and her husband. They adopted him after his mother passed. He was really close with her, but he didn't care much for her husband. He'd been trying to reach her for a while, but she wasn't answering her phone. He said that was unusual of them, but assumed they'd gone on an extended vacation as they sometimes did. I offered to get Vivian's P.I. to search the database. He declined and said he'd give them a little while longer before he put out a B.O.L.O. on them. He also said he grew up with his twin cousins that the aunt also adopted. They were like his brothers. One died in an unsolved fire, and the other was always working. So, he was pretty much by himself these days.

The more he spoke, the more I found myself falling for him and wanting to take care of him. That was one of the downfalls of being a Scorpio. We often personalize the problems of other people and try to fix them. I vowed that I would not do that ever again, but I knew that would be impossible with this man. So, I made a mental note to have Vivian run his name and to do a welfare check on his aunt and uncle.

CHAPTER TWELVE
VIVIAN

Acid Connections

A couple of weeks have passed since I saw Ava at the Queendom. The nurse sent me a text to inform that she was awake. I wasn't sure what my plans were for her, so I avoided visiting her until my head was clear. I'd been passing time with Tosha and enjoying intimate evenings with her. Things were flowing smoothly, and she finally dropped the grudge of me being Cheyenne's sister. I offered to have dinner with the three of us together to prove that I wasn't lying, but she insisted that she believed me, so I let it go. My morning jogs have been helping with the anxiety that I've been feeling. As I stretched to run the six miles of the day, Cheyenne called. I realized that I hadn't spoken to her much since the dinner at Vinny's, so I was excited to talk to her.

"Hey, Sis! How have you been?" I answered.

"Chile, I'm almost in love. Can you believe that?"

I was surprised to hear this because she's always been so private about her love life. I had no idea she was even communicating with anyone.

"Oh, really? Who's the lucky guy?" I asked.

"His name is Hakeem Blackshire. He's an ex-NBA star. I met him at Metropolis one night."

"Blackshire?" I asked as I stood up and leaned my body against my brick mailbox.

"Yeah. I know you've probably heard the rumors of him being gay. Well, I think he's just a free spirit without labels."

"Where's he from?" I asked, trying not to sound judgmental, but having a strong feeling that he was related to Tyrone and his family.

"He's originally from here. I'm glad you're asking questions because I need a favor."

"What can I do for you?"

"I need you to run a background check on him. His parents died years ago. He was raised by his aunt and her husband. I know he has a set of twin cousins, but one died in a mysterious fire. He's concerned that something may have happened to his aunt and uncle unless they're on an extended vacation."

"Sounds like you know a lot already," I joked, but I was concerned about the familiarity of those details.

"I'd love to know more about him. I really like him, so I want to help him at least find out that his family is okay. He's had a rough life."

"I gotcha, Sis. Give me a few days. I'll get Medgar on it immediately. I'm glad you've found love. Just be careful," I said with seriousness in my tone.

"If I can survive VJ, I can deal with a potential heartbreak. I love you, Viv."

"Love you, too. I'll call you in a few days," I replied.

As soon as I hung up with Cheyenne, I shot Medgar a message requesting details on Hakeem Blackshire. I also told him to run a deeper check on Tyrone Blackshire and Ava Williams Rogers. I hoped my intuition was wrong, but something told me they were connected. Instead of running six miles, I shortened it to two miles and called Tosha over. I needed to find out how much she knew about Tyrone and his family.

By the time I had showered and prepared a few sandwiches for us, Tosha had arrived.

"I guess you're enjoying our friendship," she teased as she gave me a hug and peck on the cheek.

"It's not so bad," I responded playfully.

"Look, I don't want to ruin our great time, but I need to ask you some things about Tyrone. I don't think he's really gone for good."

"Vivian, I thought we agreed to leave the past behind us. I don't want to discuss Tyrone. I'm over him and the fact that your sister helped break up my marriage. I just want to press forward with my new life," she said.

"It's not about you. I think he's connected to someone that works for me. Can you just help me, please?"

"Oh wow. Okay. Ask me anything. I'll do my best to help you."

I was relieved that she was making this easier than expected. If I had to force the information out of her, I would have.

"What are his parents' names?"

"I only know his adopted parents, Ava and Sammy. He was estranged from them by the time we got married."

My heart began to pound, but I tried to remain calm.

"Did he have any siblings?" I asked.

"He had a fraternal twin brother named Kyle who died suddenly. He investigated the case but got no leads, so they closed it as a cold case."

I instantly felt light-headed when I heard Kyle's name. Time stood still as my mind flashed back to the first time that I saw Tyrone in my office. I thought he looked familiar from the construction site, but it was because of Kyle. They had the same eyes. Hell they even favored more now that I know they're twins.

"Are you sure Tyrone's last name is Blackshire and not Rogers?" I asked.

"It's Blackshire. He kept the name of their birth parents."

"Does the name Hakeem Blackshire sound familiar to you?" I asked.

"Yeah. That's the gay NBA player, huh?"

"Yes, but is he related to Tyrone in any way?"

"Not that I know of. Tyrone never mentioned him. What does he have to do with anything?" she asked.

"I don't know, but I have a feeling that they're related."

I decided to leave out the details of Cheyenne dating him because I wasn't sure how much I could trust Tosha.

"Thanks for the information. Listen, I need to go into the office for a little bit. You mind if we hook up later or tomorrow?"

"Is everything okay?" she asked.

"Yeah, it is. I just need to go take care of something before I forget," I lied.

"Okay. Just call me later. I'll let myself out," she said as she wrapped up her sandwich and left.

I watched her through the blinds as she made a phone call while pulling out of my driveway. I wondered who could be on the other end of the phone. To be cautious, I shot Cheyenne a quick text, "*Stay away from Hakeem. I'll explain later.*" Then, I sped to the Queendom to talk to Ava. I didn't know what this bitch had been plotting all this time, but I'd soon find out.

***

I entered Ava's room with my weapon drawn and aimed at her head. She was lying in bed with the covers pulled across her face. I snatched them back, prepared to smack her awake with my gun. Instead, I found Dawn's corpse where Ava should have been. *MUTHFUCKA!* I thought as I called the crew and sent them to every known address I had on Ava. Then, I called both of my parents, but neither answered. I hoped she hadn't gotten to them before I could. I raced to Bella's place first. I didn't see her car in the driveway, but I still let myself inside and checked around to be sure Ava wasn't holding her hostage. They were nowhere in sight, so I raced to Vinny's estate. I continued to call both of my parents repeatedly. Still, no answer. I sent Cheyenne a message to meet me at Vinny's. My heart raced at the thought that I'd kept Ava alive only for her to finish her attack on my family. I just hoped I could make it to them before it was too late.

Chapter Thirteen
Bella

Love and War

After twenty years, Vinny's cum tasted sweeter than the first time we were together. I could no longer resist the urge to make love to him like we did the night I showed up at the hotel to meet him as a client. Although the circumstances weren't from a fairytale, that night was every bit of ecstasy. The way he made love to me today erased every grudge I'd ever held against him. It happened after we shared a relaxing afternoon in the jacuzzi on Bella Terrace. I showed off my figure that gave Jada Pinkett-Smith a run for her money, and he matched my beauty with his sculpted body that put Michael B. Jordan to shame. Abstinence, Vinny's sexiness, and the champagne had my hormones all over the place as I straddled his lap and felt his extremely large and equally hard dick trying to penetrate my bikini bottoms. He kissed my neck and ran his tongue along my chin and up to my mouth. We tongued like high schoolers sharing their first kiss.

The more we kissed, the harder his dick became. I caressed his beautiful hair as the bubbles from the steamy water moved our bodies around. Vinny's hands slowly made their way to my hips and then to the sides of my thighs. In one smooth motion, he lifted my small frame and removed my bottoms with one hand. Then, he placed me slowly and gently on his hard dick. The amount of time that had passed since I last had sex had my pussy tight. But in the gentlest motion, Vinny made his way inside my vagina. He lifted my body up and down slowly and sensually. My walls gripped him tightly, begging for his dick to keep its place where it belonged – right there inside me.

I felt the muscles in his arms and shoulders tighten as he continued to lift my body up and down his shaft. Just when I was ready to climax, he stood up with my arms wrapped around his neck and placed my body gently on the edge of the jacuzzi. Then, he dove his face into my pussy. His hands were no longer on my thighs. They were now in the creases of my vaginal lips near my clit, stretching it open as he sucked and nibbled me to multiple orgasms. My soft moans were nearing screams as he stuck his fingers inside my wetness and found my g-spot. He applied pressure to it as he continued to stimulate my clit. Before I could catch myself, I'd squirted in his mouth and all over his hand. He gave a sexy smile with those icy blue eyes. Then, he grabbed my hand and led me to the lounge chairs that were inside the pool near the entrance.

"How do you want it?" he asked.

"Do what you want," I replied.

"Assume the position."

I knew exactly what that meant as I got on all fours and then laid my torso down with my ass tooted up in the air. I felt Vinny's hand on the small of my back as he inserted his dick back into its rightful location. My pussy gripped him to try to stop his dick from going too deep. I could hear our phones ringing, but I refused to interrupt this much-needed and long-awaited moment.

"Relax. I won't hurt you," he whispered.

I obliged as I relaxed my thigh muscles and melted into the chair. He began to thrust slowly and steadily. I felt myself get wetter and wetter. His hands eased from my hips to my shoulders. I followed his non-verbal commands and locked my elbows with my arms straight. He began to fuck me harder as his grip tightened on my shoulders. I tried to throw that ass back, but he smacked my left cheek. The pain felt so good as I came on his dick.

"That's right, mi amour. Give it me. I want it all," he said as he continued to fuck me the way I needed.

I held steady as his hands returned to my hips while he fucked me harder and harder. He placed his thumb inside my asshole as he continued to fuck me. I came again. Just when I thought he was about to cum, I turned around, put his dick inside my mouth, and sucked it until his body began to quiver during the sweet explosion down my throat. I swallowed every drop of my man's semen, and then we both collapsed on the lounge. Our chests heaved in and out as we tried to catch our breath from the intensity of the moment.

"I love you," he said between pants.

"I know," I said as I kissed him near the corner of his mouth. "I guess we should see who's been calling our phones like a crazy person."

I grabbed my bikini bottoms that had floated underneath the lounge we shared. Then, I walked over to the table and grabbed my phone.

"Vinny, it's Vivian. She's called ten times! I hope everything is okay," I said as I called her back.

I grabbed Vinny's phone and saw that she'd called him, too. I handed his phone to him. After a half of ring, Vivian answered frantically.

"Are you guys okay!?"

"Yes, we're fine. What's wrong, Vivian?" I asked trying to remain calm.

"Ava escaped. I don't know where she is, but I think she's coming for you," she said.

"How could you let that happen? I told you to keep an eye on her," I scolded.

Vinny was standing right next to me holding the gun that he keeps in the holster that's attached to the patio table.

"I had no idea she'd shake back as quickly as she did. I found out some information on her family that I was going to confront her with, but she was gone when I arrived. She killed the nurse that I had taking care of her. I don't know if she had any help, but I do know she's missing. Where are you?"

"What kind of information did you get? I'm at Vinny's."

"Great. I'll tell you about it in a second. I'm pulling up now."

I filled Vinny in on the details of the phone call while we waited for Vivian to arrive.

"Viv's on her way here. Let's get dressed. She thinks the war has begun," I said as we headed inside.

We got dressed in the master suite and armed ourselves in case Ava was indeed headed our way. Vinny grabbed the remote and flipped to various screens on the home security system to see if the area had been compromised. Everything looked normal. Ernest was in the study, and the guards were at their posts. The chefs had been dismissed for the day, and there was no unusual activity in the history.

"Someone is helping her," Vinny said as he placed the remote on the bed and walked to the window with his weapon drawn.

"You think it could be VJ?" I asked.

"That's been strong in my spirit. I'll call the rehab to see if he's still there."

Vinny grabbed his phone and called the drug rehabilitation center where VJ was staying.

"Hi, I need to know if my son is still there… No, I don't want you to buzz. I'd actually like for you to lay eyes on him… Vincent Bourdeaux, Jr. is his name… Yes, I'll hold," Vinny said to the person on the other end of the call. "Yes, I'm still here… Great. Are you sure it's him? No, I don't want to speak him, but I do need a favor from you. Text me a picture of the person in his room and keep this between us. Can you do that? Yes, you can send it to the number showing. Thanks so much."

"Was he there?" I asked as if I hadn't heard the conversation.

"Yeah. They say he's asleep in his room. The guy that answered is sending me a picture to be sure."

While we waited for the picture to come to Vinny's phone, Vivian and Cheyenne pulled up at the same time. We hurried to the front door to meet them. They came in with their weapons drawn. Vivian looked pissed, and Cheyenne looked worried and confused.

"Could someone tell me what's going on?" she asked as we locked the door and took our conversation to the dining room.

CHAPTER FOURTEEN
VIVIAN

Unanswered Questions

By time Cheyenne and I arrived at Vinny's, Medgar had texted me the results of his investigation. My suspicions were correct about the Blackshire-Rogers family. Cheyenne asked questions as we walked up to the door of the mansion. I didn't want to repeat the story, so I ignored her until we were inside.

"Could someone please tell me what's going on?" she asked again.

I turned to Bella and asked, "Did you know Ava was Kyle's mother?"

"Are you serious?" Bella asked.

"She's also Tyrone's mother," I said as I turned towards Cheyenne. "They're twins."

"Is this why you told me to stay away from Hakeem?" she asked. "If so, what does this have to do with him?"

"Absolutely. According to this report, he's their brother, too," I explained.

"How did you miss this?" Bella asked me. "I thought you did an extensive background check on Kyle."

"I did the check on Kyle Williams. However, after Cheyenne told me to check the background of Hakeem Blackshire, I asked Tosha more about Tyrone's family. She informed me that Tyrone had been adopted and had a twin who died in a mysterious fire. That prompted me to run the check on Kyle Blackshire. Medgar's results confirm that information. Tyrone and Kyle Blackshire were born to Elizabeth Blackshire, Ava Williams Roger's sister. Blackshire is Elizabeth's married name. She was born Elizabeth Williams. She had the twins before she got married, so the state put them in her maiden name. Hakeem is their younger brother, but he believes he's their cousin by another sister who doesn't even exist. He came after she got married, which is why he has a different last name. They were too young to remember their parents who died when the twins were two years old and Hakeem was an infant. Ava couldn't bear children, and her sister and brother-in-law were strung out on drugs. So, she killed their parents and raised the children as her own.

The twins eventually found the adoption paperwork that contained the information about their birthparents. They were furious about this and changed their names from Rogers to spite their adopted parents. Kyle chose Williams to be closer to his mother, and Tyrone chose Blackshire. They never told Hakeem that they were all brothers. So, he still thinks they're cousins. For some reason, Ava never changed Hakeem to Rogers. Medgar believes she wanted to stick to the story of him having a different mother by another sister that allegedly died during childbirth. That information was included in the adoption paperwork. The twins just stuck with the original story that all of them had lost their parents and Auntie Ava and her husband took them in," I said hoping I'd made sense.

"I believe Hakeem knows more than we think he does," Cheyenne added.

"Why do you think so?" Bella asked.

"I saw our names on a list in his drawer. When I confronted him about it, he got all nervous and swore he needed it for a gift. He presented me with a painting as proof. Part of me believed him, but now I know why I still had a gut feeling."

"How did you two meet?" Vinny finally spoke.

"We met at Metropolis. He sent a drink and his number to me through the bartender. When we went on a date, he already knew I was transgender and claimed that he'd asked around about me. Do you think he could have gotten that information from VJ?"

"Or Ava," Bella said. "It seems she's been working on this plan for some time now. What are the odds of her boys coincidentally crossing paths with my children? I'm not buying that story about that nigga needing our names for a gift. Even if he did present you with something, I'm sure it's a cover up. Vinny, has that picture come through yet? If not, fuck waiting for it. It's time to mount up."

Bella's gangsta side was back in full effect. She reminded me so much of myself when Queen was ready to take over. I got it honestly, and I was proud to share that moment with her. Vinny's text alert sounded. We hovered around as he retrieved the image that came to his phone. VJ was lying in bed asleep.

"Who sent that?" I asked.

"A guy that answered the phone at the rehab. Your mother and I wanted to be certain that VJ was not with Ava. Is there any way to get in contact with Tyrone? We need to find Ava quickly before she reaches us."

"I can call Tosha to see if she can reach him," I said.

I clicked her name from my recent call log and let the phone ring until the voicemail picked up. I called a few more times and got the same results. So, I sent an urgent text message requesting a call back. After a few minutes, I called her again. This time, her phone went straight to voicemail without ringing.

"Maybe her battery died," I said. "But this is unlike her to ignore my calls."

My mind drifted back to the phone call she made when she left my house earlier, but I didn't mention it to my family.

"Do you know for a fact that she's no longer dealing with Tyrone?" Bella asked.

"Yes, I honestly believe she's left him alone. She was upset with me when she found out I was Cheyenne's sister. She actually thought I was trying to run games on her. We've hung out a few times, and she hasn't gotten so much as a text message from him. I'm certain she's innocent in all of this," I said.

I tried to convince my family as much as I tried to convince myself that my words were true. My radar never suspected anything foul from Tosha before today. I hoped my anxiety and loneliness hadn't clouded my judgment.

"Does anyone know you two are friends?" Bella asked.

"No. I hadn't even told Cheyenne. The friendship came out of nowhere, so I hadn't had time to process it myself."

"Did her name come up in the paperwork you received from Medgar?" Bella asked.

I grabbed my phone and scrolled to the page that contained information about Tyrone's life. I was astonished to see that I missed the details of him being currently married to Tosha Blackshire rather than divorced. I was too embarrassed to share that information with Bella, but I knew I needed to face the music.

"Somehow I missed the fact that they're still married. I thought they'd divorced. I wonder why it hasn't been finalized," I said as my heart pounded from anger.

I couldn't believe I'd let her play me. I'd kill her the moment I laid eyes on her.

"So, right now we have no idea where Ava is, nor can we contact Tosha or Tyrone. VJ appears to be where he belongs. Cheyenne, see if you can reach Hakeem," Vinny said.

As expected, Hakeem's phone went to voicemail as well. Cheyenne had also been played.

"Let's ride," Bella said.

CHAPTER FIFTEEN
CHEYENNE

Vigilante

Moments before Viv texted me to meet her at Vinny's, I left from paying VJ a visit. I couldn't shake the feeling that Hakeem was hiding something from me. My gut told me that VJ had tampered with my love life once again. My brother has always known how vulnerable I am when it comes to love. That's why he used my best friend to get to me. Now, he's using my new love. After my sister texted me to stay away from Hakeem, I knew that I had to take matters into my own hands. I'd learned a lot in my sessions with Bella, and I no longer felt like a novice in the game. Marissa's death enticed a hunger and thirst in me that I couldn't explain, but I knew it needed to be quenched. My mother had given me a few lethal injectables to use on unsuspecting targets if needed. However, she preferred the use of guns and knives for good old fashioned bloodshed. I swore that I'd save them for the perfect target. What she didn't know is that I had VJ in mind the whole time.

I dressed as an orderly and slipped into VJ's room as if I was administering his medication. My mouth was covered with a face mask to avoid being recognized. I wore scrubs to blend in with the staff. He was completely off-guard when I entered his room as he laid in bed laughing and talking shit to the T.V. He'd ruined my life but could lay back and enjoy a show without a care in the world. I felt myself grow angrier as I watched him for a few minutes.

"It's time for your injection, Mr. Bourdeaux," I said.

He sat up with a smile. "Yeah, gimme that good shit. You fine as fuck, baby. Won't you give me a little something extra."

The same person that gave me hell for my transformation was attracted to the very person his little brother had become. It was funny enough to piss me off even more.

"You'll get extra alright," I said with a smile. "Give me your arm."

He sat up and began to rub my leg. I cringed at his touch. I didn't want to feel my brother touching me a second longer, so I stabbed him right in the neck with the venom. Then, I watched as paralysis took over his body. I helped him lay back so that the poison could flow as needed and he'd appear asleep if anyone poked their head in his room. Then, I pulled my mask down and showed my face.

"You thought I was going to let you get away with trying to kill me?" I asked as I smiled at death coming for him.

His eyes almost popped out of his head when he saw my face.

"Yeah. Who's the queer now? Rubbing all on your transgender sister's leg. The look in your sick, pathetic eyes makes this even sweeter for me."

VJ's eyes moved, and his mouth quivered as if he was trying to speak.

"Don't fight it, big bro. Just let the venom take you out."

I gave his shoulder a soothing pat to relax him as his body slowly became limp and his eyes remain fixed on mine. I could see the faint breathing of his chest, but it wouldn't be long before he was in hell where he belonged. I laughed and sat down next to him on his bed. His lips trembled again as if he wanted to speak. I wrapped my hand around his neck and squeezed briefly before releasing my grip.

"Ha, you thought I was about to give you the easy way out. No sir, I want you to feel every ounce of pain like I felt when your friend Sammy raped me repeatedly. I want you to feel tortured like I felt my whole childhood while you got our father's love and I longed for anything he'd give me. The pain you're feeling right now ain't shit compared to my life as your brother. That's okay, though. Your little plan backfired and gave me the life I've always wanted. Our parents love me just as I am. Vivian and I have the best relationship, and I'm a part of the family business."

I stood up and walked to the door to listen for the sounds of anyone coming our way. Besides a few passersby, the coast was clear.

"One more thing… You're lucky I got to you before the family did because we each wanted to be the one to kill you. Rot in hell, you piece of shit," I said before returning my mask to its position and finding the nearest exit out of the building.

By the time I pulled out of the parking lot, Viv had texted telling me to meet her at Vinny's. I called Hakeem's number again, but still didn't get an answer. I hadn't spoken with him since our dinner date at his house a few days ago. I tried to convince myself that he was busy and would call me soon, but I knew something was off. Vivian hadn't told me why she wanted me to stay away from him. I didn't ask any questions because I knew she had a solid reason. I disposed of the scrubs and mask as I drove to Vinny's.

When I got to my father's house, my mother's car was already there. Viv and I pulled up at the same time. I immediately began to question her about what was going on, but she ignored me until we got inside the mansion. Their conversation confirmed a lot about Hakeem and how all this shit had played out along the way. I was shocked to hear some of the news, but I wasn't totally oblivious to any of it. I continued the naïve act as if I had no idea how the business worked and what we'd do next. Little did they know, I was ready for my next kill.

CHAPTER SIXTEEN
BELLA

Ava Must Die

My family loaded up our weapons in the G-wagon and began to search the city for Ava and her family. We refused to wait for her to attack us.

"I think we should go to the rehab first," Vinny said. "VJ's body looked staged. I don't believe he was asleep."

"Do you think he's dead?" Cheyenne asked quickly as she leaned forward and awaited Vinny's response.

Her question was unexpected, but it made sense.

"No, he thinks VJ could have been pretending to be asleep," I added.

Cheyenne sat back in her seat and peered out the window. I noticed a slight smirk on her face, but I didn't say anything about it.

"Surely he isn't stupid enough to come for us again after I assured him that I'd snap his fucking neck if he sneezed wrong," Vinny said calmly.

His calmness was never a good thing. I learned that quickly over the years and made sure I stayed out of his way when he became that person.

"Have either of you spoken with your friends yet?" I asked the kids through the rearview mirror.

"Tosha still hasn't texted back," Viv replied.

"Neither has Hakeem, and his phone is going to voicemail," Cheyenne said.

"Let's pay them a visit. Tosha has been renting a house in town. The address is in my phone."

"Hakeem lives off Ellerbe. We can go by there, too. I know how to get through the gates."

"Okay, but first let me lay eyes on VJ. We need to bring him with us to keep him close until we find out what Ava has planned," I said.

Vinny didn't say much as he rode with his Draco across his lap. He always hated for the empire to be compromised. It was especially annoying when the hit came from the same enemy more than once. We continued down I-49 until we reached Natchitoches. As I made a right off the exit, I saw several cops coming behind us quickly. Everyone tucked their weapons as I pulled to the side of the road. The convoy drove past us, but one of the cops pulled over behind the G-wagon.

"We've got action," I said as I reached for my weapon.

"Remain calm," Vinny replied.

I watched the cop through the rearview mirror as she stepped out of her car and adjusted her holster. She closed her car door and looked toward our way. She took a few steps in our direction and then turned around to direct traffic and allow the rest of the convoy through. As we continued to watch the cops pass, we noticed a funeral car adorned with a banner that showed a picture of an officer and his end of watch date.

We'd turned in the middle of the funeral processional for a fallen officer.

"I can unclench my ass cheeks now," Cheyenne said.

The car filled with laughter. Even Vinny let out a chuckle as we continued to VJ's rehab center. After a few more miles of driving, we arrived.

"I'll go in," Vinny said.

"We should all go," Vivian added. "We don't know who or what could await us."

"She's right," I added. "Grab your weapons."

Once everyone was strapped, we made our way inside the facility. Everything appeared to be normal. The workers were visiting patients as usual. The front desk clerk was answering the multiline phone, and the orderlies were making their rounds to administer medication. We skipped the front desk and went straight to VJ's room. I opened the door with my gun in my hand. Vinny was right behind me. The girls had the hallway secured.

I was surprised to see VJ still in bed in the same position from the photo.

"Something's not right," I said to Vinny as I pulled back the covers.

VJ's eyes were wide open, and his pupils were white with a hint of blue as if he'd frozen to death. Either he'd overdosed on cocaine, or someone got to him before we could and used the same venom we preferred for the silent kills. I felt mixed emotions at that moment. Part of me was sad that my son was dead, the other part regretted not being the one to do it.

"You good?" Vinny asked as he placed his hand on my shoulder for comfort.

"Yeah, I'm fine. We need to find Ava immediately!" I said in a shouting whisper.

"What's wrong?" the kids asked as we hurried out of the room to leave.

"He's dead," I said.

"Dead? So she got to him before we could," Vivian said.

Cheyenne forced, "Wow."

"Let's just go," I said. "We need to find this bitch."

***

Our next stop was Hakeem's house. When we arrived, the garage was up, and his car was gone. The door to his house was wide open.

"Let's check it out," Cheyenne said.

I parked in the middle of the driveway, and the family stepped out of the car together. Cheyenne led us into the house. All of the weapons were cocked and ready. Inside, there appeared to be a struggle. The kitchen was a mess and chairs were broken and turned over. The drawers were open as if someone had been rummaging through them. Cheyenne walked to the drawer near the fridge and pulled out a slip of paper.

"This wasn't here at first. Here's the sheet that listed our names for my so-called gift. There's an address and a message saying, 'Come alone.' I wonder if this is where they are."

"There's only one way to find out. Bring that with you," I said as we exited the house and headed to the address.

Vinny typed the address into the GPS system on my dashboard. As he typed, the system's voice called out each button he touched. By the time he began to type in the name of the street, Vivian said, "That's Tosha's address!"

"Do you know a quicker way to get there because this is saying twenty-five minutes. I can't wait that long for revenge. It's been twenty-five years already," I said as I bit my bottom lip trying to remain calm.

"With the new I-49 N corridor, we can avoid the traffic and lights on N. Market. Take the 220 bridge to the Texarkana exit. She lives off Myra Myrtis Road," she said.

I drove as quickly as I could without being stopped by the sheriffs along the way. Tosha's house was in the same condition as Hakeem's when we pulled up. Her garage was up, and her car was missing. Vivian led us inside to a mess that was similar to the one we'd seen at the previous stop. We'd reached a dead end. There was no note that gave us another address nor were there any other clues.

"What do we do now?" I asked Vinny.

"We wait. We can't be too anxious to move because we will fuck around and get ourselves killed. She's playing a game with us and enjoying it. Let's just wait at the mansion."

He was right. I wanted this so bad that I wasn't thinking straight. On our way back to the city, I received a call from an unknown number. I answered over the car radio.

"Is this Bella?" a feeble voice asked.

"Ava, where are you? Stop being a pussy and show yourself," I said calmly.

"You've always been eager. You were eager to take my man after I taught you the game."

"You didn't teach me shit," I said.

"I was never yours, bitch!" Vinny snapped.

"Oh, look. Hey babe!" she laughed. "Back to you, Bella. You were also eager to bury my Kyle. You passed that eagerness to your children. Vivian was eager to befriend Tosha, and Cheyenne was eager to fall in love with Hakeem. Look where this has landed your family. The Queendom has been compromised and your children have shared quite a bit of information with the people they love thanks to the eagerness passed down from their mother."

"At least I birthed my children and had something to pass down to them. Drop your location," I said.

"Calm down, little lady. We'll get to that."

"Ava, what do you want?" I asked becoming more annoyed.

"I want to kill your child like my Kyle had to die."

"You already killed VJ. Isn't that enough?" I asked.

"VJ? No, I didn't kill him. In fact, I didn't even know he was dead. He was supposed to help me again, but I needed to take care of some things before meeting with him. When we arrived, he was already gone."

"If you didn't kill him, who did?" Vinny asked.

"That's a mystery to us all," she said sarcastically.

"What was he supposed to help you with?" Vivian asked.

"Oh, he was still plotting to kill all of you. Too bad he died before that could happen. Now, my boys and I will have to take care of it. Your family has always been incompetent. You had the streets fooled, but I knew all your weaknesses, and I used them against you. Vivian, let's start with you. Power is your weakness. You love to be in control. You love to intimidate people. That's what drew you to Tosha. She was weak when she came to you, and you used that to your advantage before entering a lesbian affair with her. You killed my favorite son and then fucked the wife of his twin. Tisk tisk," she said flatly.

"Cheyenne, love was your weakness. Your crackhead mom and heartless dad failed to show you any love, so you readily accepted it from my husband and me. That's also why it was so easy for my baby boy to steal your heart. I can't believe you bought the story that he needed your family's names for a gift. Nope. He needed information on you for his mother – me. I needed him to keep an eye on each of you until I was well enough to handle you myself. Oh, and just to heal your little broken hearts, neither Tosha nor Hakeem were okay with my plans. Tosha knew about it in the beginning and tried to back out. Hakeem had no idea the extent of what I had in mind.

"Bella, your weakness has always been trying to save young women from being a drug-whore like you were. All those years you spent counseling made you weak and took you off your game. That's what attracted Vivian to me and put a rift in your relationship. She needed a motherly figure from a strong woman. That's why she kept me alive. You've never shown her your strength. All of this became too much for her, so I encouraged her therapist to suggest a friend. Lo and behold it worked in my favor when she reached out to Tosha.

"Vinny, darling. You've always wanted control. You wanted to control the streets even after death, so you told VJ everything you could think of about the game. You couldn't just let the legacy die with you. Nope, you wanted to be greedy and control everything from the grave."

I'd had enough of her soapbox speech.

"Drop your location, bitch!" I interrupted.

"Aah, the eagerness again. Meet me at the hotel where Prince Charming made you deliver VJ and Charley," she said before disconnecting the call.

"She's at the Beacon. I swore that I'd never go there again, but I need to kill this bitch. I guess you know why Tosha and Hakeem haven't answered your calls," I said loud enough for Vivian and Cheyenne to hear.

I drove as fast as I could to Bossier City. My mouth watered at the craving of finally coming face to face with Ava. I needed the pleasure of blowing her head off her muthafuckin body. When we pulled into the abandoned hotel parking lot, I expected to see the vehicle that transported Ava. However, there were no cars in sight. We sat in the G-wagon and scanned the area.

"Over there," Cheyenne said, pointing to the red laser beam that was shining through one of the motel room windows into the vehicle.

"Shouldn't we get down?" Cheyenne asked.

"Not a chance. These windows are bullet proof. They'd need an army grenade to crack them," Vinny said.

Suddenly, the room door opened and Tosha stepped out with her arms tied behind her back and duct tape over her mouth. Vivian grabbed the door handle to exit the vehicle.

"Don't you dare!" I said.

"Ma, she's innocent."

"You really believe that bullshit? Have you really gotten so weak, Vivian?"

"I've never been weak!" she yelled. "I just never got over Kyle's death. Tosha has been a great friend to me. I can't let her die because of my fuck up. I'm going to walk right in and pop Ava and end this shit."

"So you think it'll be that easy?" Vinny asked matter-of-factly.

"Fuck yeah. That old bitch could barely talk on the phone. I'm trained by the best. We can take them. Don't forget who I am," she said sternly.

"No offense, but this isn't that shit you do at the Queendom. There, you have guards and people that help you chain muthafuckas up. This is a real battlefield. We have no idea how many men she has with her. We don't know if there's one person or ten behind each of these doors," he said pointing at every motel room door. "This area alone has fifteen rooms. Can you tell me what's behind those doors?" Vinny asked.

"Dad's right," Cheyenne said. "We could easily be outnumbered."

My phone rang again.

"Come out, Ava!" I answered.

"Send my man in."

"Vincent won't be going anywhere."

"Uh-oh, she's mad now. That's the only time you call him Vincent," she laughed. "Send him in. We have unfinished business that involves this very hotel.

I looked at Vinny and asked, "What's she talking about?"

His eyes never left the door that Tosha exited.

"Answer me!" I yelled.

"This doesn't concern you, baby. I'll explain later," he said as he exited the vehicle and walked toward the motel.

CHAPTER SEVENTEEN
VINNY

It Was All A Dream

When I entered the room, a familiarity came over me as I saw Ava standing next to the bed that held two lifeless bodies. I scanned the room to see if anyone else was in there or if there were any adjoining doors where someone else could gain access. I didn't see anything of the sort.

"Throw your weapons on the bed. I know you have more than one, so please don't piss me off," she said. "Do you remember this room?"

I removed the weapon from my holster and ankle strap but held on to the one tucked behind my back.

"Why are you doing this? I've paid you for years, but you insist on fucking with my family. I never meant for that to happen to you."

"You sure as hell didn't try to stop it. You let your guys rape me and cause me to lose our baby! You didn't even care enough to get me the proper medical treatment!"

"Our baby? What baby are you talking about? I didn't have a baby with you. I fucked you one time and damn sure didn't hit raw. You could never hold a flame to Bella! I paid you because I felt bad that they caused you to have a hysterectomy at such a young age. I never wanted any of my girls working the streets forever. I wanted a few of you to have families. You also expressed the desire to have a better life. That's why I continued to take care of you."

"Don't make me shoot you. Not only did you let our baby die, but you let your step-daughter take my son away from me and then kill him," she said as her eyes began to fill with tears.

"Bella and I were no longer an item at that time. Therefore, I had no idea that Vivian even knew your boys. The first thing I knew about Kyle was when they called me to help them clean up the mess. I'm sorry that happened to your son, but I don't think it was intentional."

Ava continued to cry with the laser beam aimed at my chest.

"Who's this on the bed?" I asked.

"Those are Kyle's brothers. The only family I have left."

"Are they dead?" I asked, glancing from her to them and back to her.

"Not yet. I wanted them to finally meet their real father before I killed you and them."

"Who might that be?" I asked.

The curtains behind her had a slit in them that allowed me to see through the window. I could see the shapes of Cheyenne and Bella with their weapons drawn. Cheyenne peeped through the window. I tried to keep my eyes focused on Ava.

"You're their father, Vinny. You know you are," she said as she approached me and tried to rub my face.

I moved my head to avoid her touch and took a step back.

"You're always rejecting me," she said. "No matter how many times I've protected you and taken care of our sons along with your children with that tramp, you still found your way back to Bella and away from me. Why do you think it was so easy for me to allow your family to kill Sammy? I never loved him. He'd been in the way of my one true love for too many years. His obsession with transgender women was beyond sickening. He fed that same poison to Hakeem. That actually worked in my favor when he fell for Cheyenne. I needed each of you separate and occupied to decrease your power when I came back for you."

Apparently, she didn't know that we'd found out the truth that her sons were adopted from her sister. She may have even forgotten about the hysterectomy we'd just discussed. Or, this bitch could really be just that fucking delusional. Still, she held on the lie that I was their father. I'd never realized before now just how crazy this bitch was over the years. From the chance encounters between her and my kids to her plotting with VJ, it all made sense.

Now, I'm in the motel room where she was raped, and she's claiming that I'm the father of her kids that she didn't even birth. Furthermore, she's admitting to using her children as pawns. This war was never between our families. It was all in her mind. She wanted the life Bella had. She made herself believe that she'd shared things with me that didn't even happen. She wanted revenge for some shit that didn't even exist. I couldn't let her win this one. Before she could come any closer, I quickly grabbed my gun from behind my back and shot her in the leg. She fell to the ground. The guys on the bed never flinched.

"Vinny," she forced. "How could you do this to the mother of your children?"

Just then, the door to the room opened and Bella walked in. She kicked Ava in the face and blood filled her mouth.

"He's not the father of those fucked up ass kids, bitch! You're not even their mother!" Bella shouted as she repeatedly kicked Ava. "What did you do to my son!?"

"I told you that I never laid a finger on VJ. When we tried to get him after Tyrone helped me round up Tosha and Hakeem, he was already dead."

Cheyenne's face showed signs of guilt each time VJ's death was mentioned.

"I trusted your old ass, and you were playing me all along. You even convinced me that my mother was too weak to train me properly and that your strength could make me better. But I knew she was strong and taught me enough to handle business. Missing Kyle threw me off my game, and I fell for your lies. I can't believe I was so fucking dumb. Let's take her to the Queendom," Vivian said. "The guys have a hot bath waiting for her and her family."

Within fifteen minutes, the crew had arrived and loaded Ava and the two bodies into the van. Tosha was still tied up. Vivian and Cheyenne each held on to one of her arms.

"What are you going to do with her?" I asked Vivian.

"Throw her in the back with them. I don't trust this bitch either," Bella said.

Tosha tried to moan something but the gag in her mouth muffled her words. Vivian's eyes seemed sympathetic.

"Vivian don't fight me on this. Your judgment has been off for quite some time now.

You admitted it yourself. Throw her in the back with her family and let's ride!" Bella scolded.

Without hesitation, Cheyenne and Viv released Tosha's arms. Paul swooped her up and placed her in the van with Ava and the guys. My family returned to the G-wagon and followed the van to the Queendom.

"Cheyenne, you killed VJ," I said. "That's why you've gotten so silent each time the subject came up."

She stared out the window and allowed me to speak.

"Didn't I forbid you from touching him until your mother gave the go ahead?"

"Look, y'all have no idea how that asshole tormented me my whole life. I've always wanted him dead, but I never had the guts to do it. Now, I'm stronger than ever before. You're damn right I killed him! Just like Bella taught me!"

"Is this true, Bella? Did you train Cheyenne to do this behind my back? I thought we had an agreement," I said.

"I trained Cheyenne to protect herself against the enemy. I had no idea she'd be bold enough to kill VJ in a secured facility. I'm actually quite proud. I'm just glad Ava didn't get the pleasure of doing it, but it was high time that VJ was gone. He was no good for this family. I can't believe I birthed a disloyal, evil piece of shit like him," she said with a blank expression on her face.

That was the end of that conversation. Bella felt how she felt, and Cheyenne got the revenge she deserved. We rode in silence as we all prepared our minds to end the war with Ava.

CHAPTER EIGHTEEN
THE QUEENDOM

War: What Is It Good For?

When everyone arrived at the Queendom,
the crew transported Ava and her family to the
room that held a large tub filled with acid. Tyrone
and Hakeem had awakened, and Ava was in and
out of consciousness as she'd lost a lot of blood.
Tosha was full of fear as she continued to moan
and cry for Vivian's sympathy. The crew sat Ava's
family in the four chairs in front of the tub.

"What's the play, Ms. Vivian?" Paul asked.

"This one's up to my mother. Remove the gag from Tosha. I'd like to hear her explanation before we move any further, though."

Paul removed Tosha's gag, and she immediately began to plead her case and beg for her life.

"Vivian! I would never work with this bitch to bring any harm to you! We shared so many amazing moments together. You know what Tyrone did to me. His mother gave me so much hell during our marriage and even helped him hide the cheating. When I thought I wanted to reconcile our marriage, I reached out to her like a fool. She played on my emotions and made me believe she was sincere in helping me. She eventually told me about the scheme against your family, but I refused to help her. I didn't tell you it was happening, but you know I was very open with information about his family." Tosha said. "When I left your house earlier, I called her to make sure she wasn't going to go forward with it. She assured me that she was over it all since I wouldn't help. The next thing I know, they're at my house tying me up and shit."

"You told me you were divorced. Why do the records show that you're still married?"

"I had no idea his mother knew the judge in our case. They never filed the paperwork. Once she injected her sons at the motel, she told me that she'd make it look like I went crazy and killed Tyrone and his family in a nasty divorce settlement. I didn't know her connection to your family at first. You've got to believe me, Viv! I'd never do anything to hurt you intentionally," she pleaded.

Cheyenne walked up to Hakeem and slapped him.

"You're a sick ass liar just like this old hag! I almost bought that lie about the gift. I didn't dare want to believe that you'd been working against me the whole time. You're obsessed with women like me just like your sick ass father. I hate you!" she said as she spit in his face and smacked him again.

Holding his jaw, Hakeem explained himself to Cheyenne. "Chey, you gotta believe me. This shit was all Auntie Ava's doing. When she first presented me with your picture, I thought she was just trying to be supportive of my attraction to women like you. She did mention that she wanted information on your family, but she said it was on a business tip. I thought she's was talking about house-flipping or some shit like that. I had no clue of this lifestyle. You know I've been away for years between college and the NBA. After all the shit I went through with the rumors, I was just glad to have someone understand my desires. Then, I met you, and you were amazing. I was finally able to live freely without judgment. If I had known she was sick and on some revenge shit, I would never have agreed to get any information on you. The gift was sincere. You love your family like I love mine. I just wanted to do something nice for you – even if I got the information in a foul ass way. I'm sorry, Chey."

Tears began to fall as Cheyenne stepped away from Hakeem and took her position next to Vivian. Vinny stood beside his family waiting for Bella to come to a decision.

"Paul, go ahead and throw this washed up, wrinkled, deranged, barren-womb slut in the basin. She has fucked with my family for the last time," Bella said. "Tyrone, you may join her."

Ava's limp body dangled as Paul and one of the guys grabbed her and tossed her into the boiling acid. Her body immediately started to dissolve. Then, they grabbed Tyrone and threw him in as well. He struggled, fought, and cursed at Tosha and Vivian until his body met the acid that had erased all traces of his mother. Hakeem and Tosha sat silently as they awaited their fates. Neither said a word. They just wept at the thought of melting away for simply loving two people and ending up in the middle of a revenge war.

"Should we let them live?" Bella asked walking over to Vinny who stood silently and allowed his family to get the revenge they deserved.

"Use your intuition, Bella. Ava's gone now. What would the old Bella do? Do you trust your gut? Do you think they will continue to be a problem? Do you believe their stories? Think, Bella," Vinny said calmly with his hands gripping both of her shoulders.

Bella stood in silence for a moment before walking to her children.

"What do you two want to do? As much as I'd like to throw them in the basin with their family, my gut is telling me they're innocent. At this point, it's up to the both of you," she said.

Cheyenne and Vivian looked at each other then back at Bella before looking at the people that had their hearts.

"Vivian, it's your call. I love Hakeem, but I love my family more. If you think they should die, let's handle this right now," Cheyenne said.

Vivian walked over to Tosha and kneeled down to meet her eyes. She didn't say a word as she stared into her eyes to see her soul. After she found her answer, she walked back to Cheyenne.

"I believe Tosha is telling the truth. Do you trust Hakeem?"

"Yeah, I do," Cheyenne said as she stared at the gentle giant. "I don't think he knew what Ava had planned."

"Let them live," Bella said.

"Good call," Vinny agreed.

Vivian and Cheyenne walked to their lovers and embraced them as tears flowed. Vinny and Bella hugged and then led their family back to the parking lot. They watched as their children and their lovers loaded in Vivian's Audi that she kept parked at the Queendom. While the crew cleaned up yet another mess, Bella and Vinny got into the G-wagon and rode home with a sense of peace that Ava was no longer a problem.

REVENGE:
THE SWEETEST JOY

Written by
Viv Love

About this Guide

The following questions are intended to
enhance your group's reading and discussion
of Viv Love's

REVENGE:
THE SWEETEST JOY

DISCUSSION QUESTIONS

1. Who's your favorite character? Why?
2. Who's your least favorite character? Why?
3. Who has the most control between Vivian and Tosha?
4. What do you think of everyone's reasons for revenge?
5. What did you think of Vivian in this story versus her role in *Daddy Issues* and *Thy Queendom Come*?
6. What do you think of Bella compared to the character she displayed previously?
7. Do you think Cheyenne is built for the family business?
8. Do you think the family should have let anyone live?
9. Do you think the new love connections will work out?
10. Were you shocked by the plot twist?

More books by this author:

Daddy Issues
Thy Queendom Come

Available in paperback and e-book

Order at
www.valpughlove.com
or
www.amazon.com/author/valpughlove